DRAGON'S CLAIM

RED PLANET DRAGONS OF TAJSS BOOK NINE

MIRANDA MARTIN

CONTENTS

CHAPTER ONE

PENELOPE

a lock of hair is sticking to my face, and I blow a huge puff of air at it, trying to get it out of my eyes. I'm not entirely successful, but I don't want to stop to free up my hands until I make it to Ormarr's apothecary. Putting the heavy box of herbs down and then picking it back up will only be more effort. I can deal with an irritating lock of hair for a little longer. Even in this heat.

It's the middle of the day, which means Tajss's twin suns are beating down on me without mercy. I squint so I can at least see where I'm going. Falling now would just be icing on the cake. Plus, I wouldn't want to have to fish everything out of the sand on top of everything else.

The herbs I'm carrying are an early harvest. With Bashir's help, Ormarr's been able to get some basic flora going, simple plants that can take care of simple needs. But the box I'm transporting now has the big guns, herbs I'm sure he'll be excited to see. As soon as he gets his hands on them, I know he'll be itching to brew some new tonics.

Of course, I have to get there first.

The heat is intense, and I'm near full exhaustion from

running water out to the men periodically to make sure *they* don't get dehydrated as they work on the wall. Probably I should have kept a better eye on my needs as well. I take a deep breath and trudge forward. I will not pass out. That would be way too embarrassing. So I won't.

I try to think of something else to distract myself from the weather and the burn in my muscles. My mind wanders to the wall, and I immediately wonder if one of the dangerous creatures on this crazy planet will show up and damage it before the men even have a chance to finish it. Judging from previous experience, chances are that is exactly what will happen.

I sigh as I adjust my burden.

Maybe that sounds pessimistic, but I think it's actually realistic here.

I really would have liked to enjoy this planet we ended up crash-landing on, but it's difficult for me to get past all the negatives, even when everything is relatively quiet like it is now.

There are so many things on Tajss that can kill you if you aren't careful. Plants, animals—even a disruption in the supply of epis that keeps us humans alive, giving us unnatural resistance to the harsh conditions here. This place has some of the most gorgeous flora I've ever seen—and the ship had records of quite a lot of plant life. But does it really matter how visually appealing all of it is when most of the plants can and will kill you, given half a chance?

Vegetation is supposed to be the safe kind of life!

And the animals here...they're some of the most awesome examples of beasts, which is definitely the word I would use for the majority of them. But, again, they aren't even close to being safe. It's an approach-at-your-own-risk kind of deal. Many of them would kill you rather than look at you.

Even if one wanted to tranquilize them to conduct some

scientific study, many of them have thick hides that a normal dart can't even begin to get through. So tranquilizers are useless. Probably worse than useless. You'd probably only succeed in irritating the heck out of the animal and causing it to attack.

I adjust the box again. I'll have impressive muscles in no time at this rate. Hey, maybe I'll end up looking as badass as Sarah Connor in *Terminator 2*. I can only hope. I blink as sweat drips into my eye.

Ugh. Not worth it!

Honestly, what I find most difficult to understand about all of this is how the men talk about Tajss, specifically how everything was here in the past. When it was a civilized planet, before the war that destroyed their entire way of life. They talk about all the wonders of the glory days, but, at the same time, they act as though those days are gone forever. Like they can never be recaptured.

Why?

Why do they think Tajss cannot be redeveloped, cannot again become that wonderful world they remember so fondly? They were able to do it before. Why not again? It's as though they don't even want to try! I simply don't understand that mindset. Embracing such a bleak and fatalistic idea about future development is much too depressing for me.

And resigning myself to living here as it is? Without any hope of improvement? I can't think too long about that or I'll really sink into the doldrums. I'm having a difficult time just living moment to moment as it is. Maybe that's why I'm the only one who is holding out hope that there might still be a way to get off Tajss.

Maybe it's desperation—okay, it's probably desperation. But it isn't completely out of the realm of possibility that Earth fared better than Rosalind thinks. Maybe there is a way to communicate with home. I can't just let that go. I'm too stubborn a person. For a lot of situations, I truly feel like if there's a will, there's a way.

If anyone has the will to try for this particular dream, it's me. I don't even care if it is a desperate hope. The truth is, I need that hope. Even if the others may think it's delusional to hold on to it. I need that delusion to keep going. To keep living in this place like this.

It's not because I'm not grateful. I fully and completely appreciate the hospitality the Zmaj have shown. There's no denying the fact that we'd all be dead if it weren't for them. If it weren't for these gargantuan hunks with hearts of gold. They saved us. And for that I will always be grateful.

This just isn't the life I want to live.

Maybe it does sound like I am ungrateful for this new chance at life, but it doesn't change how I feel.

I still miss what I lost. I had a career on the ship. I inspired and molded young minds after years of studying for that position. I felt like I had a purpose, like I made a valuable contribution to our community.

And here? Here, it's just—

My train of thought cuts off as a huge bird-like creature sweeps by the wall, its predatory, sharp-featured face signaling it's no gentle beast. I watch it warily as I keep moving, but it continues on without making a move to gouge anyone's eyes out. Whew!

The animal sighting has me mentally shifting gears back to my book, a Tajss encyclopedia I've been working on, a project that keeps my mind engaged. It gives me something to do so I don't go completely crazy here.

"That is a vtak," Ormarr explains. "Though I have no idea why it is out at this time of day, when the suns are still high in the sky. They tend to hunt at night unless there is a storm coming."

I grunt, making a note of the name as I lower the sizable box to the floor, careful to use my legs and not my back.

"Why did not one of the men carry this here?" Ormarr asks, frowning. "It is much too heavy for you."

Really? I cock an eyebrow at him.

"If we can carry your babies for eleven months and then go through labor, we can definitely handle hauling a box," I retort, placing my hands on my hips as I catch my breath. It was difficult to lug the thing around. But no way I'm going to admit that now.

Ormarr smiles, like he can see what I'm holding back, the amusement dancing in his eyes as he heads over to lift the herb box.

He picks it up easily—the weight is obviously much easier for him to carry than it was for me—and takes it over to his sturdy work table.

Muttering to himself, he sorts through the bundles. Lifting a sprig to inhale its fragrance, he hums under his breath as the scent hits him.

"Good harvest," he remarks, setting it down with care. "These will certainly come in handy." He smiles at me. "Thank you for your work, Penelope. It is much appreciated."

I give him a small curtsy, ready to head back out.

I'm so sweaty and sticky from being out in this heat. I know exactly where I want to go next. Though it might be some time before I can get away.

"Wait." I turn around, frowning as Ormarr stops me. "Take this with you," he says, holding out another sprig, this one smaller than the other.

I hesitate at the mischievous glimmer in his eye, taking the offering slowly.

"What's it for?" I ask warily, wondering what the joke is.

He chuckles at my suspicion.

"Simply for fragrant bathing," he reassures me. "No drying

required. I believe you will enjoy the experience. I've heard some of the women complaining about the lack of supplies."

I tense, hoping my dismayed reaction isn't noticeable. Does he know about the spring I found? Why else would he give me this? And have that look in his eye?

I can't ask without giving it away, and I need that place, need the tranquil solitude it provides. Sometimes I feel like it's the only thing keeping me sane here. I scan Ormarr's features. There's no way to know for sure. If he does know, something tells me he won't rat on me. He could have already if he knows. And he hasn't. As far as I know.

That last sequence of thoughts confuses even me.

Shaking my head, I search his eyes, but Ormarr's are hard read. He'd probably be an excellent poker player. Deciding to err on the side of caution, I put on my game face. If he isn't going to broach the subject directly, neither am I.

"Thank you, Ormarr. That's really very thoughtful of you."

He inclines his head at me, a smile still flirting with his mouth as he turns back to the herbs.

An hour later, I still haven't gotten a chance to escape. I sit, watching Delilah trying to reformulate her secret sauce. It was legendary on the ship. I know I'm not the only one hoping she'll be successful sooner rather than later.

"I just can't seem to get the right proportions," she mutters to herself, the table in front of her covered in samples of various non-lethal flora, as well as smoked and powdered meat bits. It's quite a daunting array of potential ingredients.

"I'm sure you'll get it," I encourage her. "That last batch was definitely closer."

She nods, muttering something else to herself as she scurries over to the pot again. A lot of us have taken to various endeavors to keep our brains engaged here. Delilah's sauce is probably the equivalent of my encyclopedia. Something to focus on, something to keep her sane. As I watch her lose herself in her self-imposed task, I realize this is the perfect opportunity for me to slip away. The others are engaged in their brain-defrags. No one will miss me. So that's exactly what I do.

Quietly, I leave the village, trying not to draw attention to myself as I make my way over to my secret spring, where I'm sure nobody will bother me. I feel a little twinge of guilt as I make the trip. I'll probably let the other girls know about it eventually, but I feel like I'll snap without a little more time to myself. At least for now. There's just so much to process, so much to reflect on. I need to decompress to keep my mind sharp, keep myself in balance. The grind of day-to-day life in a place like this can be mind-numbing all on its own. So I'm okay with keeping this small pleasure to myself right now.

A woman has needs! Not the least of which is a greater purpose, at least for me. If I all I can have is this small pleasure, I'm going to hold onto it as long as I can.

I wipe the sweat off my forehead as I continue, pondering what my next step should be in terms of finding an intellectual outlet for myself. The hand-written starter encyclopedia I've been filling out with the information I've gleaned from the others is a good start, but I'm nearing the end of what I can accomplish with that. I'm reaching the point where I'm going to be ready to explore the wild with a purpose, to gather more intelligence directly to add to my project. It feels like the logical next step.

There's just one problem with that. I'm not stupid enough to think I can handle myself out there alone, immersed in Tajss's wilderness. I'm a casualty waiting to happen on my own. And doesn't that just chafe?

I've never felt so completely vulnerable.

On the ship, I knew I could handle myself. Here, it's an entirely different story. It hasn't sat well with me since day one. It's so frustrating to feel like I can't even take care of myself, especially since I'm so used to being able to do that.

To make matters worse, none of the men will help me improve, help me become more self-sufficient. They won't train me to hunt, won't train me to fight. Both things that I firmly feel like women need to know how to do on this planet! What will we do if something terrible happens and we have to fend for ourselves? No way we'll be able to survive for long without being able to at least find food for ourselves. The Zmaj are proving stubborn on this. But I'm stubborn too. I'm going to keep chipping away at the obstacles put in front of me because I'm not giving up.

But for now, I'll settle for striking a deal with one of the Zmaj to help me venture out of the camp and write the manual. I'm not an idiot. I'm not going to head out there alone only to be eaten by the first animal—or plant!—that thinks I look tasty.

I sigh. I've been sighing a lot lately. Man, I really hate feeling helpless. It's more than annoying in this environment —it's terrifying. I ponder that until I hit the small rock wall and settle back into the present. I don't want to think about all that right now. This is supposed to be my time to relax, not think about everything driving me crazy. I have the rest of the day to do that.

I take a deep breath, the fragrance of the herbs growing nearby making me smile. The spring—my own private hot tub—is tucked safely behind the short wall. The water sparkles in the dappled sunlight. My tiny oasis from the harsh world.

I have an urge to jump in immediately, feeling every sweaty, gritty moment of being out in the hot sun, but I take my time, glancing around to make sure nobody else is in the vicinity. When I'm sure the coast is clear, I can't undress quickly enough. When I'm bare, I slide right into the warm water. It's always the perfect temperature. Thankfully, today is no exception.

Closing my eyes in pleasure, I take a minute to enjoy it before reaching for my clothes. I fish out the sprig Ormarr gave me, adding it to the small bit of unscented soap I still have from the ship. Oh, it smells amazing! I inhale deeply, reveling in the water and that delicious scent as I soap up, getting the grime of the day off me. I feel like a new woman afterwards. This is exactly what I needed.

Thank you, Ormarr. You're an amazing man—er—dragon.

I roll my eyes at myself, soaking in the delicious moment. I let myself relax, let my body drift onto my back, enjoying the sense of weightlessness, the warm water cupping my body...

Wait.

What's that sound?

My eyes snap open as the heavy, rapid footsteps close in.

It sounds like someone is...running.

A big someone.

Who is—

A big Zmaj clears the small wall in the next second.

My train of thought freezes as my eyes meet Bashir's own startled ones.

Oh, shit.

His eyes glance down at my breasts for a split second, revealed from my floating position on my back. I gasp, immediately using my arms to cover myself, feeling the blood rush to my face.

Tajss, why do you hate me?

He looks just as embarrassed as I do, quickly averting his eyes.

"Excuse me," he mutters, turning and promptly running away again, almost with more speed than he'd used to get here. He must have heard me and come to investigate. Maybe he thought I was in trouble. I don't know. But no matter his intentions, the damage is done.

I sink lower in the water, though it's no use now. I'd been so careful. So careful to dress modestly, to avoid any hint of romantic interest with any of the Zmaj. I'd maintained dignity and respect, not wanting to be seen as a potential partner in a relationship. But that is all likely gone now.

Not because I'm the most beautiful woman in the world, but even *human* men are visual creatures. And Bashir is more sexual than that—he's one of the big, lusty dragons for goodness sake! I'm more than likely sexualized in Bashir's eyes now, and there's no going back from that. No matter how many loose clothes I wear now, or how businesslike I keep my demeanor, you can't go back from being seen naked.

Letting out a frustrated huff, I let my arms drop. What's done is done. I don't relish seeing Bashir again. I can already imagine how hard it's going to be to look him in the eye without blushing. It's going to be weird, but I'm going to have to just push through it. Maybe if we both ignore what happened... Damn it, why did it have to be Bashir out of all the Zmaj?! I have to see him every day!

Mood completely shattered, I wade to the edge of the water and haul myself out to get dressed.

Well—

At least he was a gentleman about it.

CHAPTER TWO

BASHIR

$\mathcal{I}$ peel another root vegetable and hand it over to one of the humans volunteering to make dinner tonight. It is a small contribution, but it's all I have the energy for at the moment. Working on the wall has been exhausting. The physical effort and long hours are taxing on all of us, though we hope the end result will be worth all of that. I pass another vegetable on.

A communal dinner will be a nice way to unwind, especially after Drosdan's battle with the worm. It struck fear in the humans' hearts, and they're still afraid. Tajss is a harsh planet with many dangers. The humans are obviously not accustomed to living in a place with danger, or anything less than complete safety and a climate-controlled environment. Their bodies alone would have been a clear indication of the luxury of their lives even without their reactions to danger.

An image of Penelope's blush-pink nipples flashes through my mind, the picture crystal clear. It has appeared in my mind an inordinate number of times all day, along with an accompanying flash of heat I cannot control. The delicate curves of her breasts with the sparkling drops of water glimmering in the sun. The perfect circle of surprise her lush lips formed when she realized I was there, the hue nearing the exact shade of her nipples.

Her spring-colored light blond hair wet and slick against her head, leaving her pretty face bare and drawing attention to her large, verdant green eyes. The short hairstyle is apparently called a "pixie-cut", or so I've been told. I simply know I adore it on Penelope, enjoy how it exposes the elegant curve of her long neck and shows off the delicate contours of her face. I want to touch that soft neck, graze her lips with mine. Feel every part of her. The image of her bathing has plagued me relentlessly, my arousal not ever abating completely.

The worst of it is that I know she was horrified to be seen like that.

She had thought herself alone, secluded. I would never have intruded upon her like that, but I'd heard what I'd thought was a sound of distress. I hurried over to make sure someone was not in need of help. Now I wish I could take that moment back.

I do not take pleasure indulging in a physical response to her stunning beauty when she did not share herself —willingly share herself—with me. It cheapens the act that it was something stolen. There is a way things are done, and it is not like this. I will accept only a fully willing mate, one who desires me as much as I desire her.

To that end, I've deliberately waited to find a mate among the survivors, the one female who is mine. It's been Penelope I've found the most beautiful, both inside and out. Yes, I appreciate her height, her lithe build, her attractive features.

What's even more important is that she has shown herself to be intelligent and strong-willed. She is a fierce thing, all that fire clear behind her clever eyes. Were she not also such a soft thing, I would have trained her to hunt and fight when she voiced her desire to learn both.

She has a warrior's heart and the persistence to match.

She has been pestering all of us to teach her, though on Tajss, every Zmaj has two shadows—I mean, we all agree. It is simply unthinkable to knowingly expose her to that level of risk. One wrong move would end her life. That is unacceptable when she is a sure treasure—*someone's* treasure. As she will be, when she finally relaxes a bit and allows herself to be protected, to be cared for like she deserves.

It is obvious she resents needing help from the way she bristles when it is offered and refuses to ask for it until it's necessary. She is going to have to make peace with the fact that she always will need help. Here, it is a necessity to work together. Tajss's reigning natural law is immutable—the strong and adept survive. The reality will always be that working together ensures our strength, ensures the continuation of life here under these extreme conditions.

Penelope still lashes out when she needs assistance, spitting out sharp words. But she needs assistance just the same. It will be easier on her and everyone else if she simply accepts that fact and works with it. It does not mean she is weak; simply that she is another piece of this whole we are creating together. She is still struggling with the concept, and it is painful to see. I do not want her to be unhappy.

My time among the humans has shown me that my ability to read people is not isolated only to the Zmaj. They wear their suffering in different ways, but the truth is always there if you know how to look for it. Just like with the Zmaj, humans must also accept their condition before anything can truly change for the better. It is an inevitable truth that we all must face.

With Penelope, I can almost see the ideas flow through her mind, reflected in the flare from her bright eyes. I hope she won't be let down too harshly when she finally accepts her fate here. I do not think she will. There is something in the resilience of her spirit that makes me think she will bend and not be broken. A strength that I see shared among those that have been able to make a life here.

She certainly has a brightening effect on my day. Even if she avoids meeting my eyes for long and leaves the vicinity quite quickly.

She's always keeping herself busy and writing in her book. In fact, the longest period of uninterrupted time I have spent with her so far was when she interviewed me about the garden. She looked so enthusiastic and alive as she scribbled about the herbs and fruits, asking questions about their various properties and methods of preparation.

Her cursing when her pen hiccupped ink made me smile, though I tried to suppress the inclination. I did not want her to think I was laughing at her. Her eyes were as determined as a bivo's as she recorded her words on the pages, her focus clear. I had hoped the interview was the opening I needed so we could converse with each other, become more familiar. But as soon as she was done asking me questions, she was off to pull Melchior to the side and mine him for data as well. It was disappointing, though not all that surprising.

Ormarr later told me that Penelope was a teacher on her ship, which gave me a better understanding of her character. I know it must be difficult for her to stop using her mind for everything, as she was accustomed to doing before her ship crashed here, but she needs to learn how to adapt to her new way of life. It is not going to be like the one she enjoyed on the ship. Clinging to that memory will only make the transition more difficult.

She might learn to enjoy life on Tajss more if she spends a little more time exercising her spirit and her soul as well as her brain. She needs to learn to enjoy life here, or it will be very long for her indeed.

Her ship was destroyed.

There is no leaving Tajss now.

Why not learn how to make the best of circumstances? Sometimes, I have the feeling that she is fighting against the world. A useless endeavor. Doesn't she realize she does not have to be alone here? That she can make this life easier for herself?

I look up as Penelope comes in again, carrying more of the roots. She gives me a quick smile and a nod before she disappears back out to the garden. She has been in and out, helping set up, but I have the feeling she's deliberately avoiding staying here. This time, she doesn't come back with her book in her hand until dinner is ready.

Then she avoids my eyes as much as she can. She is definitely uncomfortable around me now. It is not how I want her to feel about me.

I wish I had not stumbled upon her at the spring. I frown, looking away, feeling discouraged by this setback that was no real fault of my own. I'm wondering how I am going to fight past it, when I catch her peeking at me while Melchior launches into a tale of impressive bravery, with the others chiming in.

"And then the bivo charges—"

"It was the biggest I've ever seen!"

"He was going to be trampled to death!"

I don't look directly at her as the story continues, wondering if...

There.

She glances over at me again, the action furtive, before opening her book and pulling her pen out, her face focused as she begins to scribble again. Like an infant Zmaj crouched behind his father, she hides behind her growing encyclopedia. Perhaps that is my opening, an avenue I can use to engage her, spend time with her, learn if we share the same feelings.

Nothing else has worked so far. And letting this awkwardness linger between us does not feel like a good idea. I do not want her to solidify this emotion between us, always associate me with embarrassment.

All right. I shall ask her about her book. Taking an interest in her interests will hopefully get me back into her good graces.

I continue to watch her discreetly, not wanting her to realize I am doing so. I do not want to scare her away even more. She scribbles quickly as the information flows around us, right up until the topic turns to Sarah's condition. She puts her book down to listen attentively, leaning forward in her seat. I see the flash of worry and anger cross her face. She's angry that Sarah is hurt, and she's right to feel that way. It was so unnecessary after her and Drosdan's sacrifices to help the New Villagers.

The mood is somber after that discussion topic, the food nearly gone. This is the best opportunity I am likely to have. I tense, ready to go over to Penelope and broach the subject of her work—

But before I can even get up, she hops to her feet and calls out a general goodbye to the group before she hurries away.

I sigh silently.

Too late.

I soothe myself with the fact that at least I have a plan of attack now, one I will employ as soon as I see the opportunity. I know exactly what I want to ask. I want to know if she has recorded information about her planet as well, and if she is willing to share it with me. It is perfect. A topic I have a genuine interest in and one that she seems to as well.

I hope I will have a chance to broach the subject soon.

I am patient.

I will proceed with care.

CHAPTER THREE

PENELOPE

I take a deep breath as I carry water out to the guys again. It's fine, I tell myself, just act normal. My eyes instantly pick Bashir out of a whole group of Zmaj working on the wall outside. I literally can't help being aware of him. My heart picks up its pace.

The sun is glaring down on him, glistening off the sheen of sweat covering his muscled body. His beautiful scales reflect the light in a rainbow of colors as his body flexes with the tough physical labor they're having to do out here.

I swallow hard. For a moment, I completely lose myself in the broadness of his shoulders, in the flex of the muscles of his back. I want to run my hands all over that beautiful skin—

Get ahold of yourself woman!

I shake my head, trying to regain the composure that I lost as soon as I saw Bashir. I shift my gaze away hurriedly as I walk over to him. He's dangerous, at least to me. Maybe it'll help if I don't look directly at him. I offer him the water, my gaze still averted in self-defense.

"Thank you," he murmurs, the deep tone of his words sending another shiver of awareness through me.

This is ridiculous. He's just a person. I look up briefly and accidentally meet his eyes. The look in them tells me I did not avert my eyes quickly enough earlier. He saw me staring. The knowledge is there in his eyes. I look away immediately, hoping he thinks the heat is responsible for the flush I feel on my face.

Damn it. I've been so careful!

What is it about this man in particular that has managed to sneak under my guard like this? When there are equally attractive, well-muscled specimens literally all around us. It can't be because he saw me half-naked. We're both adults. As mortifying as that was, it wasn't the end of the world. No, it has to be something else. Something about him just...draws me in. Something more than his body, as gorgeous as it is.

I find myself trying to figure out what he's thinking. What's going on behind that still face as those intelligent eyes take in everything around him. My mind goes into overdrive worrying at this question like a dog with a bone, trying to understand him. Trying to understand my response to him.

I risk another glance at him, watching the muscles in his throat work as he guzzles the water. A trickle of it escapes his lips and slides down that smooth skin... I lick my lips involuntarily, completely avoiding his eyes as I take the water jug back and hurry away, going back to the well as fast as I can.

It's downright embarrassing how much he affects me. I can't even retreat and avoid the situation. Everyone has to pitch in, and I'm not going to admit that I can't do my job because I can't spend time around him. So I end up having to suck it up and spend half the day running water jugs over to the Zmaj, including, of course, Bashir.

I won't complain too much about it. I have a close-up view of exactly how much they're busting their asses to get this massive example of Zmaj craftsmanship finished. I sincerely appreciate it, along with everyone else. Our lives depend on the defense it will provide. My personal problem with Bashir is nothing when compared to that. So I put my head down and keep going.

On my third run from the well, Bashir manages to stop me from making another quick getaway. So close!

"How is your book coming along?" he asks, wiping sweat off his brow, his eyes appearing genuinely interested.

I soften a bit at the question. That's really quite thoughtful of him to ask. And he look like he cares about my answer. Maybe he hasn't lost respect for my intelligence just because he saw my naughty bits. Maybe I haven't been giving him enough credit.

"It's coming along," I respond, letting myself relax a little. The topic steadies me, puts me back on sure footing. This is a subject I can navigate.

"I hope you'll share it one day," he says, a small, charming smile crossing his face.

I blink, distracted at how it transforms his already-handsome face. I wrestle my mind back onto the right track. I shake my head, taking a step back.

"I don't know how to write in your script—" I hedge.

"Maybe you could read it to me then," he interrupts, easily circumventing the obstacle I've thrown out. Refusing to be deterred so easily.

I bite my lip as I realize he's flirting with me. There's no way to deny it. Not with the way he's watching me, the amount of effort he's putting into conversing with me.

Part of me likes the feeling of being desired by someone like Bashir. It's flattering. I'd be lying if I said I didn't feel a flutter inside. But another part of me doesn't like it. Doesn't want to muddy the waters like this. Not when I know I don't want to mate.

Erring on the side of caution, I shrug, giving him a noncommittal smile.

"Maybe," I say breezily, deliberately acting as though I don't realize he's flirting. I retreat right after that, before he can come up with another way to delay my exit. I need to get out of there before the conversation slips completely out of my control. I avoid his eyes the rest of the time, not giving him an opening to continue the interaction, though I know I'm not really fooling him.

The retreat is as much of an acknowledgment of what was going on as a direct response would have been, but it buys me time and space, at least for now. Time to regroup.

The thing is...I could feel the sincerity with which he approached me. Like he wants to really get to know me, not just on the surface, but the real me. He didn't seem at all like he just wanted to get into my pants. It's...unexpected.

Maybe it isn't fair, but the image I've formed of the Zmaj men in general runs counter to that. Their idea of mating seems pretty restrictive. Like a gentle prison where the guard cares about you and takes care of your acceptable needs. No thanks. I've valued being my own person for too long to fall into that trap.

One thing my parents' split taught me was that I don't ever want to be part of a set that can break. And they can always break. My mother's own experience was a harsh learning lesson for me. She never really recovered emotionally after she and my father broke up. And my father...well, he just had a full midlife crisis party with the women who'd been eyeing him on the ship. The callous disregard for the woman who'd spent years with him was not a good look. I lost all respect for him and for the institution of marriage.

I've distrusted even the idea of love ever since. As an

adult, I wonder about how realistic it really is. Passion and chemistry definitely exist and they're nice to experience. But does that giddy feeling really endure? I doubt it. I think people stay together more out of habit than anything. Until one of them finds something more exciting, and then the other is just shit out of luck.

But that doesn't mean my mind isn't still preoccupied with Bashir, even though I know better. That night, when I go to my room, he's all I can think about. How his eyes watched me. How they seemed to look right through me, past the careful face I present to everyone. Right to *me*, the me that I keep under wraps, protected from the world. It was disconcerting. His genuine curiosity and interest definitely got under my skin in a way I didn't expect. He's different than the others. Enough so that it makes me wonder...

Maybe it wouldn't be so terrible to date him, explore what this is, chalk it up to experience and move on. Get it out of my system. I roll over in bed, sighing. I can't do that. It isn't an option. Not when I consider the fact that the Zmaj mate for life. It would be cruel to lead Bashir on when I know that isn't what I want. I can't act on this odd draw between us. So I'll have to do my best to put it out of my mind instead.

What I don't realize is that others might be noticing the interplay between us. I know I act differently around him and that he does the same, but it isn't comfortable to have that pointed out by someone else.

"You're being kind of weird around Bashir," Delilah mentions out of nowhere while we're out in the garden.

My head whips around so fast, I'm surprised I don't injure myself. She gives me a probing look, wiping the sweat off her gleaming dark skin. Shit. I feel the panic rise. What do I say? I run through maybe twenty responses in a split second before settling on a classic—denial. I can't handle the truth.

But Delilah is no dummy. Swallowing, I muster up the lady-balls to tell her she's wrong.

"Weird?" I repeat, frowning. "No more weird than around the other Zmaj." I shrug casually, hoping I'm not overdoing it.

Delilah raises her eyebrows, clearly not buying what I'm slinging. But she just shrugs and drops the subject, going back to working the garden.

I'm glad for it, but I also feel like I just succeeded in alienating her by not being truthful or confiding in her. Delilah isn't the super-sensitive type, but we have developed a bond. One that hasn't gone deeper yet simply because it's difficult for me to let people fully in.

Letting my guard down where my feelings—or non-feelings—are concerned isn't easy. I don't like people to have the power to hurt me, which means I've never been like other girls, bonding and making friends easily. It's not natural for me. I'm mostly a loner. I never learned how to deal with other people when I've messed up, like I just did. I don't know how to fix this right now without giving too much away. I hesitate, thinking of and discarding overtures that feel stiff and unlike me. I finally give up and let the slight feeling of distance lie. Maybe it's for the best. She won't ask any more personal questions.

Delilah's question does make me more cognizant of the fact that people around here notice things. There aren't so many people that it's easy to overlook how everyone interacts. Very inconvenient, but there's no help for it when you're living in a tight community like this. The best I can do is just act like everything is fine, stick to my routine, and try to limit my exposure to Bashir. The less time I spend around him, the less people will have to read into. I don't know if I can act completely normal around him, so that's my best bet.

I manage to do just that for the next several days, leaving when I see him coming, only speaking when necessary, avoiding eye contact. If only it was so easy to limit him from my thoughts! I'm having an impossible time trying to shake him from my mind, and it's damn irritating! I like being in charge of my mental space. A lot. Being in control there is comforting when I feel like I don't have a heck of a lot of control in other parts of my life right now.

Even more frustrating, I've taken to avoiding the spring. I just can't see it as the same oasis of peace it was before...the incident. In fact, I guess I might as well tell the other girls about it now. It won't be a place for me to unwind again for some time to come. I'm in my own head the rest of the day, brooding about everything. Same with the next day.

Right up until I hear raised voices. The anger in them is clear. What's going on, I wonder, along with everyone else in the vicinity, and we all run over to the wall to find out. I stop at the edge of the gathered crowd, watching Padraig snarl at Melchior.

"You do not want to fight me," Melchior snarls back. I can see from his stance and heated eyes that he too is ready for a physical altercation.

The two Zmaj men are circling each other, rage blazing in their eyes, obvious in the way they're holding their bodies. The Bijass has taken hold of them both.

I don't know how to stop—

I gasp along with everyone else as they collide with each other, hisses and growls punctuated with blows as they grapple.

"Shit!"

"What do we do?"

"They're going to get hurt!"

"Someone, do something!"

"Enough!" Bashir barks out sharply, his voice loud and authoritative. It actually gets through to the fighters.

23

The two break apart, though it looks like it is simply to take a breather rather than any real desire to stop the fight.

Bashir closes in on the pair, striding forward with a purpose and steps right between them, seemingly unafraid. That's a very dangerous place to be right then.

I take a step forward before I stop myself. My getting in there as well won't help matters. I'm much more breakable than any of those three. One good punch from a Zmaj fist and I might not get up again.

"There is no reason for this," Bashir murmurs when he has their attention, his eyes meeting Melchior's. When he sees Melchior focus on him, he turns to meet Padraig's eyes as well. "No reason."

Melchior looks like he's backing off the edge a little, but Padraig is still breathing hard, a red mark along his jaw from where the other Zmaj got a hit in.

He probably deserved it. Padraig has had a thorn in his side for weeks. Snapping and snarling, being short with everyone who has the misfortune of being around him. It's getting on *everyone's* nerves. If ever there was a candidate for a Zmaj who needs a mate to tame him, Padraig is it. He's a poster child for sexual frustration if I've ever seen one, though it doesn't excuse his behavior at all. The other Zmaj without mates aren't snapping people's heads off.

We all watch as Bashir looks back at Melchior, taking in his calmer demeanor. I can see him make the judgment that Padraig is the more dangerous one.

Melchior gives him a small nod and takes a step back, signaling he is done with the fight.

Bashir turns back to Padraig, giving him his undivided attention now. Padraig still has his hands balled into fists at his sides, his head lowered, looking at Bashir in a way I'm not comfortable with, like he's just itching to mess him up. I wish Bashir would put some distance between the two of them...

"You can control this, Padraig," he murmurs, lowering his voice, meeting that rage-filled glare without flinching, his own eyes deliberately calm. "You are not your Bijass."

I frown. There's something about the way Bashir is looking at Padraig. His eyes are looking deeply into him somehow. It sounds crazy, but that's the only way I can think to describe it as he continues his low, almost hypnotic murmur to the Zmaj. Like he's not just talking to Padraig on the exterior. But also...his inner dragon?

It sounds so stupid when I say it like that, but... Padraig's fists slowly loosen at his sides. His stance slowly straightens from that combative crouch. His eyes start to clear. Bashir is getting through to him!

I let out the breath I wasn't even aware I was holding, watching Bashir calm Padraig so much more easily than Drosdan did. I don't know how he does it, but he manages to diffuse the situation without resorting to anger himself. It's definitely impressive to watch. As Bashir lays a careful hand on the other man's shoulder, he's self-possessed and commanding without having to reach for his Bijass. I can't take my eyes off him even as the crowd starts to disperse.

Bashir, you just got a hell of a lot more interesting.

CHAPTER FOUR

BASHIR

"The wine is done fermenting," Melchior remarks. "Perhaps we can break early today and enjoy it. Tajss willing it will be a beast-less night."

We all murmur our approval as we continue working on the wall, the suns beating down on us in their usual merciless manner. I wipe at my brow as I stretch my back. Halting work a little earlier than usual sounds nice, but that is not why my heart skipped a beat at the suggestion of a night of socializing.

Green eyes flash across my mind—Penelope's eyes. She hasn't been far from my mind all day. The idea of being able to speak to her in a more relaxed atmosphere certainly has its appeal. It could be the very opportunity I need to break through more of her shell to find the woman underneath. She is always attempting to shield that woman, to hide her spirit behind the ever-capable mask she wears at all times. But I've seen peeks of her, and I want more.

Hope has begun to bloom in my heart the more time I spend around her, the more I learn of her. There *is* something between us. Thoughts of her have taken up much of my internal dialogue, and I cannot help but wonder if it is the same for her too. Her behavior tells me that she feels the draw just as I do, especially the way her gaze lingers on me when she thinks I am not looking. But I want to hear it in words. I want to taste her desire for me on her lips. I know the wait will only make the moment sweeter between us, though it is painful to delay it.

Thoughts of Penelope have the rest of the workday passing by in a blur, the distraction enough that I do not even realize we are done until one of the others taps me on the shoulder. I clean up quickly in preparation for the evening, attempting to maintain my composure. I do not want to scare her by being too eager or pressuring her too much. I already know she does not respond well to being pushed.

She likes to be in control.

I deliberately show up somewhat late so that I can see where Penelope is seated. I smile at her and sit down close enough to converse, but not so close that she might feel uncomfortable. She gives me a wary look but relaxes as nothing else happens.

Does she think I will bite her? Hmm. I have several places in mind already that I would like to sink my teeth into. But only if she asks.

The wine is passed around. I murmur my thanks before sampling a sip of it. Not bad, though I do not think it would win any awards if we had more choices.

The carefree mood, the wine, the fact that we are done with work for the day—all of it contributes to a more relaxed atmosphere as the conversation grows louder. Penelope appears more relaxed as well.

Perfect.

"Penelope," I venture. She turns to me, her guard a little lower than usual, her cheeks pink. She looks lovely, a little mussed, her hair ruffled from her fingers. "I am curious about your planet. Perhaps you could indulge me with some of your favorite Earth songs?"

Her face softens further, a smile lighting her face. Ah. Perhaps this is the way to her heart. She cannot seem to resist the opportunity to reminisce.

"Oh, there are so many," she responds, her face brightening even more as she turns fully towards me. "Let's see...maybe I should start with some of the basics. The Beatles had quite a few hits..."

I listen intently as she lists various songs.

"Are you talking about the Beatles?" Delilah asks, wandering over. "I have to say, my favorite is when Paul McCartney sang 'Maybe I'm Amazed,'" she confesses, sighing, obviously taken with the song.

I see a few more of the humans perk up as they listen in on the topic. It seems to be a favorite.

"'Maybe I'm Amazed'?" I repeat.

"Yes, it's great!" Delilah clears her throat. "I'm not a great singer, but I'm willing to give it a go." She takes a deep breath. "Maybe I'm amazed—" she starts, her voice a little bit shaky.

But the other humans familiar with the song quickly chime in, bolstering her. Delilah is modest. Her voice is true, and the way she sings is heartfelt and moving.

"—at the way you love me all the time. Maybe I'm afraid of the way I love you..."

I listen to the words, the melody. It is pleasing to the ears and obviously a song for a loved one. I like even more how much everyone seems to enjoy it. I look over at Penelope, who is now grinning from ear to ear. Perhaps this is an opportunity I should not let go to waste.

I stand, and she looks over at the movement, a questioning expression on her face.

"Will you dance with me?" I ask with a smile.

She looks a little warily at my hand. If she refuses, I will simply have to—

But she places her hand in mine and stands. My smile widens as I pull her into a dance, a slow one that allows me to hold her close. Though I don't know if it could really be called a dance when we are simply swaying to the song. I do not care. I have accomplished the goal of getting her into my arms.

The room falls to a hush around us as people see me dancing with Penelope, but Delilah pokes one of the others with her elbow, and the singing starts up again.

I am in her debt.

When I look back at Penelope, her face is showing some self-consciousness at being the center of attention, but that does not last for long. Soon, others join us on the dance floor, and those singing switch to a different song.

Penelope relaxes a bit more in my arms, and I pull her that much closer to me. Her cheeks flush a deeper pink when her eyes meet mine, but she does not pull away. She is too relaxed to reach for her shields as quickly as she usually does.

"Is this still the Beatles?" I ask, enjoying the feel of her slim body in my arms. Having her this close is a kind of torture, a torture that I do not want to end.

"No," she says, smiling. "This song is by a band called Journey. Here, let me show you how to dance to this..."

I let her guide me, finding the movements easy enough. I like the dance. As I genuinely like the music. Though perhaps it is simply Penelope I like, and I enjoy her pleasure in this. She makes the Earth seem fascinating. Just like her.

My heart is beating fast. A trickle of sweat is sliding down my back, though the temperature is not too warm. It is the feel of her lithe body willingly pressed up against me—it is almost too much for me to process after watching her from afar for so long. But I manage to keep my calm front intact. I do not want to scare her away now.

She retreats into her shell so easily when the fear of whatever is holding her back rises. I want to know what that fear is that stops her from reaching for anything more—but I will not push. I will never push. I will wait until she is ready to tell me.

So we simply keep dancing. Our bodies rubbing against one another. Our eyes locked. The room fades around us, until it is only us and the swaying of our bodies. The heat—I know she must feel it too—is rising between us. I want this moment to last forever, but nothing perfect ever does. Eventually, the singing comes to an end, and the rest of the world reappears around us. Penelope steps back, her expression dreamy as she gives me a shy smile. I smile back. I could have danced with her forever, but the moment is broken as people begin to talk again.

"Do you guys want to learn how to play checkers?" Delilah asks as we all linger, not ready to end the night. We are all enjoying ourselves too much.

"What is check-hers?" Padraig asks with a frown.

"It's a game. Here, I'll show you."

Delilah runs and grabs a piece of natural chalk, and we all gather around as she draws a grid pattern on a flat, raised rock she deems appropriate for the lesson.

"I'll teach you guys how to play chess once you get the hang of this," she explains. "Chess is more complicated and requires more strategy, so checkers is a better game to start with."

The other Zmaj and I watch as she takes some berries and separates them into two piles of different colors. The bitter and the sweet. I watch and listen as she explains the rules, along with the other Zmaj unfamiliar with the game. Interesting. It seems simple enough.

"Who wants to play first?" she asks once she's done, looking around.

"I would like to play," Melchior offers, looking interested.

"All right," she agrees with a smile.

We all gather around to watch as they play. The rules seem simple enough, but there is obviously some forethought required. Melchior's brow furrows as the game continues, but he does not manage to beat Delilah.

There is some strategy to learn after all. The women all cheer as she wins, but Melchior is not upset.

"This is fascinating," he says, smiling. "I shall practice to improve."

"We should adopt this game," I agree, wanting to play as well.

"I can create a true game board, with playing pieces that are not food," Arawn offers, grinning at the berries. "I must say though, I appreciate Delilah's ingenuity."

"That would be great!" Delilah says with an answering grin. "We can use the same board for chess, though we'll need different pieces."

"When can we learn this other game?" I ask, intrigued. "Chess, did you say?"

She chuckles.

"Once you guys are good at checkers," she explains. "Hold your horses."

I do not know what horses are or how to hold them, but I can only assume she means to practice patience. This I can do. My eye strays to Penelope now that the game is over. My patience has already been tested and proven.

As I watch, she makes her way to the wall, swaying a little, no doubt in response to the wine she drank earlier. She moves over to the unfinished portion of the structure, leaning her small hand against it. She tilts her head back, drinking in the twinkling stars and silvery moon. The soft light caresses her face, highlighting the delicate bones. For a moment, I almost see the child in her, filled with wonder, unguarded, innocent, unafraid, simply absorbed in what beauty there is to be found on Tajss. Likely she'll feel differently once the effect of the wine fades, but I love to see her like this. With her thorns temporarily removed, exposing the softness I knew lay beneath.

She turns to meet my gaze as I venture closer. I have a moment where I wonder if she will rebuff me, but she does not. In fact, the exact opposite happens as I come to a stop near her.

I go completely still as she reaches a hand up to cup my cheek. It is the first intimate gesture she has initiated. Anticipation buzzes in my blood as I soak in the small touch.

"You're a nice dragon," she says with a small smile, her words slower than usual.

I smile back. She is clearly deep in the wine.

"I aim to be," I respond, amused at the openness of her without her shields. "Kindness is a virtue I hold dear."

"And handsome," she adds, tapping my cheek with one of her fingers. "You are handsome, too."

I feel my smile turn into a grin.

"Thank you."

She nods, turning her sight back to the stars, her hand dropping. I reach out to turn her gently back towards me. I cannot resist. Just one kiss, here under the stars. After she has touched me so sweetly...

I lean close, waiting to see if she desires what I do. Her eyes fall to my lips, and she leans towards me as well.

Yes.

Passion beats in my blood as the distance between us closes... Her breath whispers across my lips... My eyes drift closed.

"Bashir!" Ormarr calls out to me, his voice cutting right through the gossamer threads of that magical moment.

I stop, a breath away from Penelope's lips, cursing internally. But I cannot ignore the healer. Penelope frowns at the interruption.

"Yes?" I call out, straightening.

The moment has been lost.

"We need you here." A brief pause. "Penelope should come too."

CHAPTER FIVE

PENELOPE

*O*rmarr's voice is like a bucket of cold water. The buzz I have going from the wine immediately dissipates as Bashir steps back, obviously unhappy at being interrupted.

I'm not.

I'm relieved. I wanted to kiss him. That I could admit, at least to myself. But it would have opened up a whole can of worms I'm just not ready for. So what if I'm a little disappointed? This is for the best. I'm just going to keep reminding myself of that.

I'm so distracted by my internal dialogue about what just happened, I don't even realize who is standing next to Ormarr until we're almost upon them. Next to him is a beautiful woman, with long dark hair and a strong presence.

A potent mixture of confusion and excitement jolts through me. Being summoned by Rosalind is not a usual occurrence. Having her show up in person... A twinge of worry colors my emotions. The Lady General is a busy and important woman. Why is she here?

"Hello," she greets us, even her voice sage and strong, that of a self-assured woman. Sometimes I feel as though she is the perfect role model—calm, composed, intelligent, decisive. Bashir and I murmur our own greetings as I wonder if she ever has moments of doubt. Perhaps she simply hides it better than the rest of us. She smiles at us now.

"Ormarr has been generous enough to allow me to go through the starter tonics he has brewed so that I may take some back to the apothecary."

"You are always welcome to medicine," Ormarr says, nodding at her.

" I appreciate that," she acknowledges.

This cannot be the only reason she is here.

She could have designated the task easily enough. She might be going through the tonics, but Ormarr no doubt advised her of what would be most useful.

When she turns back to us with a purpose, I know I am correct. We've only been standing there for a minute perhaps, but I already feel the suspense building.

"That is not the only reason I am here, as I am sure you have guessed." She looks between Bashir and me. "I came to recruit you two for an important mission—I believe you are both the best candidates to send to the New Villagers to represent us and help forge a relationship."

What?

I'm set back on my heels by this. The possibility wasn't even on my radar. She thinks we'd be good representatives for something so sensitive?

I share a glance with Bashir, who looks equally surprised. I turn back to Rosalind, trying to conceal my negative reaction.

"Can I ask why you think so?" I venture carefully, then add quickly, "though I *am* flattered at being chosen..."

"No need to appear so shocked," she responds with a of humor. "Bashir here makes for an excellent diplomat—I've seen how he deals with the other Zmaj." That was true enough. I'd witnessed it myself. He's very good at remaining calm and calming others, a good trait to have when negotiating anything. "He is also a good protector and guide." Bashir inclines his head at her. She turns to me. "And you, Penelope, you are someone I hope they will trust. It will be a good thing for them to see that you have accepted life with the Zmaj, that you can live side by side with them even after your past experience with abduction."

That all sounds plausible, but I'm distracted by something else. There's a suspicious knowing gleam in Rosalind's eye when she looks between Bashir and me. Can she guess? Is it so obvious, the tension between us? Did she see how close we were to kissing? Or am I reading too much into a simple look?

This will drive me crazy.

I brush it off. Even if she suspects something, it doesn't matter. I've recovered my head, and I won't be acting like a lovesick schoolgirl with Bashir anymore. I'm done. I plan to take this mission very seriously. Rosalind can trust me.

"This is an honor," I finally say, overwhelmed at being chosen for something like this, something so critical. "I will do my best."

"I'm sure you will," she agrees gently.

As she gives us the details of our new positions as ambassadors to the New Village, tasked with extending an olive branch, I try my best not to let my awe of General Rosalind distract me from focusing. I just feel so honored. Honored, and also embarrassed at how easily I let my dignity slip with Bashir. I will not make that mistake again. I need to be more like Rosalind—devote myself to what needs to be done, keep my mind on duty. I need to prove to myself that I can do this, that I can be a valuable member of society here.

We don't have a lot of time after we are hit with this

news. Bashir and I immediately start to pack and ready ourselves for the trip. This isn't something that can be put off. Rosalind wants us to make the journey back to the city with her and her attendant in the morning. Which means there also isn't much time to think about what we're going to be doing, something that is almost a blessing in itself. It means I don't have time to feel too much anxiety.

The journey is boring—something I am grateful for, honestly. Boring is good. Boring is safe. I can be friends with boring.

When we arrive at the city, I spend a little while taking it in. It's an example of what Tajss used to be, what the Zmaj were able to create at one point. Before the Devastation, before the series of events that set them back to the Stone Age as a civilization. Yes, there are broken windows and twisted steel, lending an air of past tragedy to the place. But it proves that they had the know-how, had the technology to build something so advanced and impressive. It also means it could be done again. I know it can.

Rosalind moves forward and punches in the code to let us in through the protective dome, the first door and then the second closing behind us.

The processed stone feels a little strange under my feet after walking on the sand outside for so long. People walk around, going along with their day as we arrive, some calling out greetings to Rosalind. She acknowledges them as she speaks to us.

"I think it would be prudent for you two to speak with Sarah before you leave," she informs us.

"I think you're right," I say, and Bashir nods, so that is our first stop.

I don't know what I'm expecting when I first see Sarah, but it isn't to find her so healthy and doing so well. I feel a rush of gratitude as she greets me by running over and throwing her arms around me. She's doing so much better than the word around the tribe was suggesting!

"You look great!" I exclaim as I return her hug.

For a while there, we all thought we'd lost her. I've never felt so good about being so wrong.

She laughs, ending our hug with a tight squeeze.

"I feel good," she agrees, rubbing her round belly. "And it's good to see you too! How was your journey?" she asks, including Bashir.

We chat a bit, getting caught up with things, but the talk quickly turns to why we're here.

"I have directions to give you," Sarah informs me. "But I'd also like to make a request—I miss my kedi and I would like it back, if at all possible."

Kedi? I look over at Bashir, completely confused as to what she's asking for.

"We will bring the creature back," Bashir agrees, before looking over at me. "It is a small and furry creature. Harmless," he says. "A pet."

"Picard is a sweetheart," Sarah reassures me, her eyes imploring. "Please?"

"Of course," I agree, patting her hand with a smile. Small, furry, and harmless are all words I can get behind. "We will make it so," I say with a twinkle in my eye.

She laughs in response, shaking her head at the reference.

"I really appreciate it."

Then she gets down to business. I take out my book and take careful notes, drawing a simple map with the landmarks she describes. It's a vast desert out there. When you're traveling, sometimes mile after mile can look exactly the same. Details are important, so I make sure to record all of them, even the ones that don't seem so important right now.

"...I think that's about it," she finally says, sitting back.

"Great," I say, taking another look at my notes before closing my book. "Thank you so much Sarah."

"I'm glad to help. Come visit again—maybe when you don't have something this big to stress over."

I chuckle, standing.

"Yeah. I will."

Bashir and I say our goodbyes and leave her to go about her day.

"She seems much better than I would have expected," Bashir remarks as we head out.

"Yes," I say curtly.

He gives me an odd look before sliding back into silence. And not a companionable one. I feel a twinge of guilt but strengthen my resolve again. I've been trying to keep our interaction on a professional level, not engaging more than necessary. Maybe I'm a bit sharper than I was, but I need to keep him at a distance. The sooner he realizes that's what I want, the better off we'll be in the long run.

When he doesn't show up to dinner later that night, opting to eat in his quarters instead, it's clear that he's gotten the picture. I manage to annoy myself by missing him, but I suppress it. This is for the best. We need to limit familiarity with each other.

Even though I accept that on an intellectual level, images of Bashir are all I see in my mind's eye when I try to sleep that night.

"Damn it," I mutter to myself, turning over again, punching my pillow in aggravation. It's stupid, but I feel frustrated and irritated that *he's* decided to stay away from *me* now. As if only I should have the control over whether or not we spend time together. Immature and childish, but there we have it. I am, apparently, immature and childish when it comes to Bashir. My behavior so far certainly supports that theory. I slam my eyes closed. I have to just let it go. I need my rest.

Tomorrow, we're going to set out for the New Village. Travel can be grueling on Tajss. It will be no picnic, to say the least. I know that. But try as I might, sleep does not come easily. I finally fall into a fitful, light slumber that doesn't leave me feeling like I've slept much at all.

The lack of sleep does not help my mood in the morning. Not that it matters. We have to leave on schedule.

We set out from the city early, before the suns are high in the sky and the day is at its hottest.

"Have a safe trip," Rosalind says, there at the exit from the domed city of Draconis to see us off.

"Thank you," I murmur, turning toward Bashir. "We'll try to make good time."

"I'm more concerned that you are successful in opening up communication channels with them," Rosalind says.

"We shall put forth every effort," Bashir reassures her gravely.

And that's it. With one last wave, we leave the dome. We're off to the races—or the New Village.

I open my book, going to the first step in the directions Sarah provided.

"Are you sure this is the correct direction?" I ask as we start walking.

Bashir looks over at me, his eyes flicking down to my open book. His mouth tightens as he sees my notes.

"I know how to navigate on Tajss," he says, a slight hint of condescension in his tone. He turns away again and continues walking.

All right then. I roll my eyes.

We keep walking, taking a turn at a grouping of rocks.

"Is this the correct one?" I ask, looking over at it skeptically. "Sarah said it looked kind of like a moose." I squint at the rocks. Maybe if I tilt my head a little...

"These are the only rocks in sight," Bashir says, forced patience in his tone. "Whether or not they are shaped exactly as described does not matter as much as the location."

I look around and realize he's right. There's nothing else to compare to.

When I look back at him, he's staring at me, his gaze sardonic. I nod, moving forward briskly. A hear a sigh escape him, can almost feel the frustration coming off him in waves. Irritated myself, I glance over at him as we keep walking.

I completely lose my train of thought when my eyes land on his bare arms, his muscles gleaming in the sunlight. Whatever rippling is? That's exactly what they're doing—and doing it well.

Focus!

I look away quickly, back down to my book. It takes a while for the lines on the paper to enter my eyes and make shapes in my brain that eventually turn into words with meanings, but I do finally manage it as we keep walking.

I hate the desert. That must be what's messing with my mind. It sucks the life right out of you, the unrelenting suns and the miles and miles of sand. At least it looks like we're making good progress so far. That's some consolation.

"There—we shall travel to the right of that oasis," Bashir announces, pointing the way.

I look up. Sure enough, there's another landmark. I glance down to read the snippet about it as we near.

"I shall lead," Bashir announces, his eyes watchful as he steps ahead.

I feel irritation rise again. No, he is not going to just commandeer the mission here. I won't let him. I step ahead of him deliberately.

"I'm capable of leading," I counter, hurrying forward. "And

there aren't any signs of danger that I was warned to look out for."

Bashir lets out a frustrated huff of breath.

"You do not know—"

"I have the route right here in my encyclopedia," I interrupt him, waving the book in my hand as we reach the oasis. "Don't even worry about—"

I let out a short scream as Bashir's hand closes on my arm, and he pulls me back sharply. My hands automatically grip him, adrenaline pumping through me hard at the abrupt pull. It takes me a moment to realize how close I am to Bashir.

Really close. Definitely too close. I can feel him all along my front, our bodies almost vibrating against each other at the contact.

As soon as I realize it, I take a large step back, trying to summon the indignation I should be feeling at the manhandling.

"Why did you—"

"You were going to walk into that cvet," Bashir admonishes me, pointing. "I thought perhaps you would like to remain whole."

I follow his gesture to the large fleshy plant with the orange and red center, its big leaves shivering slightly. Swallowing, I take an even bigger step back this time. Cvet are carnivorous. They secrete a paralytic poison and then digest their prey. If it hadn't been for Bashir, that big one would have gotten me, all because I was focused on my book and not the environment.

"Oh," I mutter, trying not to freak out at how close I was to disaster. Needing something to do, I crouch down to pick up my book. I'd dropped it when Bashir had yanked me back.

"What are you doing?" Bashir asks suspiciously.

I take a deep breath, flipping through the pages.

"Trying to orient myself on the map," I say.

I don't want him to see me as dead weight, as a useless addition to this trip.

"I know another route," he counters firmly.

I look up at him, scowling.

"Sarah went to the trouble of describing exactly how to get there—"

"It's useless now," he interrupts again. "Do you see that rock formation over there? We're supposed to use that path at the base."

I follow his arm to where he's pointing and see exactly what he means. There is no path. Rocks fill what must have once been a way through the large grouping. There must have been a cave-in at some point.

This time, he doesn't bother to say he will lead, and he doesn't ask me to follow him. He just starts moving forward, assuming I'll follow. Frustrated and embarrassed, I hustle to reach his side.

The worst part is I know he's right about everything he said.

It's damn annoying.

CHAPTER SIX

BASHIR

I understand Penelope's desire for control, but relying on a book instead of me in this case is utterly ridiculous! No amount of words on a page are worth more than actual experience, not out here in Tajss where dangers lurk around every corner. It is not as if I do not know where we are going.

Her constant doubts and second-guessing are irritating me to no end. I tried to be gentle with her, but she has proven to be hardheaded. She is quiet now as I lead the way, and I know she is not happy with how I have handled things.

Tough.

She almost walked right into that cvet because her nose was buried in the pages of her encyclopedia. I will only humor her so far, and safety is a hard line. I will lead for her safety and mine, and she will simply have to come to terms with it. I glance over at her, seeing the hard set to her jaw and the sweat she wipes from her brow as she keeps walking with determination.

I soften somewhat.

She is not made for Tajss. She is attempting to control a

situation she is simply not equipped for. Sighing, I turn my eyes forward again and continue walking—

The sand explodes in front of us, the impact of something hitting the ground reverberating underneath us. Small rocks are shooting from the sky itself, tails of fire trailing behind them as they fall towards the ground, the whistling noise made by the speed at which they are traveling reaching my ears. They are rushing towards us. We don't have much time. Shelter. We must find shelter now.

I turn to Penelope. She is frozen in shock, staring up at the sky.

"Pardon me," I say quickly, not waiting for an answer before I scoop her up and easily settle her onto my shoulder. She lets out a squeak.

"What are you doing?" she demands, her body stiff in my hold. I start to run as fast as I can. In this case, her feelings will have to wait.

"We must find cover," I say grimly.

Then there is no more time to talk, all my energy taken up with avoiding the molten rocks slamming into the ground around me. Sand stings my eyes as one hits just a few feet away, the impact leaving me stumbling for a moment, but I recover quickly. Growling with effort, I launch myself forward even faster, using my wings to leap long distances, twisting in midair to avoid the meteorites.

They are coming more and more quickly. Soon I will not be able to dodge them at all, as they will come down in a denser pattern. One hit to either of us and we could be dead. It wouldn't matter how small the rock was—they are going too fast.

Gritting my teeth, I push every ounce of speed out of my body. I must get Penelope to safety, whether or not she is truly *my* treasure. I am not as hopeful as I was. She certainly does not trust me until I insist upon it, and that is not the way I prefer to engage with people. Certainly not my mate. Perhaps she is not mine after all. I just barely pull myself back before another rock hits the ground, driving home the point that I must focus on the present for now. I know a semi-adequate shelter nearby that we may be able to reach, a shallow cave that is much better than being in the open like this.

Somehow, I make it through the falling rocks and to the shelter with Penelope, without being hit. Breathing quickly, I carefully slide Penelope off my shoulder.

"Are you well?" I ask, scanning her body to be sure. "You were not hit?"

She nods, her face pale, eyes full of fear as she looks back the way we came. I look too, seeing the shower of rocks now hitting the ground. Too many. If we had not found shelter so quickly...

I take a deep breath, growing concern in my gut. Meteorite showers are unprecedented on Tajss. There have not been any in *millennia*.

"Maybe...maybe this was why that nocturnal bird was out so early. Ormarr mentioned they act like that when storms are brewing," Penelope remarks, her voice shaky.

I make an agreeing sound, distracted by my own thoughts, hearing her almost from a distance. When I focus on her face, I can see my worry is increasing her own sense of unease. There is no point in worrying her further. We need a distraction. Food is always a good one, especially in times of stress. It is as good an idea as any.

"I will cook. We may as well eat while we must remain under shelter," I say in a level voice, attempting to project calm as I move to open my pack.

She nods, her eyes leaving the meteorites to watch me.

There is already a fire pit ready to go, no doubt left by the last Zmaj who took shelter here. I quickly start a fire, stoking it before I take out some of the meat we brought with us.

"Have you seen meteorite showers here before?" Penelope asks as I set the meat over the fire to cook.

"No," I respond. "This is the first time. I do not think there has ever been record of another."

"Hmm." I hear her scribble something in her book. "How did you know about this place?"

"It is a shelter often used by traveling Zmaj," I explain, attempting not to let my irritation at her fascination with her book show. I can see she is nervous and trying to cover the emotion, but those pages cannot fix everything.

"What about the bird? Do you think..."

She trails off as she finally looks away from the page and up at my face. Perhaps my irritation at the questions for her book are showing, because she clears her throat and closes it instead of finishing her question.

Glancing over at the meat, she moves on to something else.

"Is there something we can use to flavor the meat?" she asks hopefully, looking over at me.

Relieved at the practical question, I immediately go on the hunt. The cave is shallow, with an extension built in front to expand the small enclosure. In a back corner, I find some dried herbs left in a basket, carefully preserved. I take them out, smell them, rub the leaves between my fingertips. They are safe, meant for cooking.

"We can add these for flavor," I explain, rubbing my find on the meat.

She nods, stepping closer to watch. I can see she's holding her tongue, wanting to ask more questions for her book, but she does not ask them. To avoid irritating me? I grin at her.

"Would you like to know what it is?" I tease.

Her face lights up and she nods enthusiastically, letting

her questions burst out. I answer them, enjoying the animated look on her face, curiosity deepening her gorgeous eyes. Suddenly, I find I do not mind the questions so much. It doesn't take long for the meat to cook, the herbs adding a delicious fragrance to the small space as our voices parry back and forth.

"Smells good," Penelope remarks with a smile as I hand her a piece.

I nod, taking a serving myself.

"What kind of food did you have on Earth?" I ask, curious as I bite into the meat.

She swallows her own bite before continuing.

"Most of what I know is from movies and television shows," she admits. "Fiction. But we had approximations on the ship. I particularly liked fried chicken—a type of bird coated in batter and cooked in oil. Not the healthiest of food, I'll admit, but really very delicious." She tilts her head to the side. "But that's only one kind of food and Earth was a large planet with many different countries and cultures. My favorite kinds of food apart from the chicken were Chinese food, Italian, Mexican...I really miss salsa."

I could hear the true longing in that last bit, and I did not want her to dwell on it. She could not change her location after all.

"What else did you have on the ship?" I prod, wanting to move her on to something happier.

Her face brightens immediately.

"Oh, we had games, different from chess and checkers—games you play on a screen. Ones like *Mortal Kombat, Halo*..."

She continues to talk about the fun ways to occupy time on their ship—a necessity, I am sure, since they could not go outside. The light from the fire flatters her pretty face as she continues to chatter happily. The smell of the food, the soft light, her memories of the ship, all of it improves the mood, distracting us as much as possible from the meteorite showers.

She is so enthusiastic about her memories of the ship, I find myself wishing I could see it in all its glory. Perhaps play a game of *Mortal Kombat* with Penelope. It sounds utterly ridiculous. I wonder what it would be like to have metal arms. Or four arms. How much more could I do with double the arms? An odd but interesting thought.

Once we finish eating, I set up a pallet for Penelope so she can be comfortable.

"Thank you," she murmurs when I tell her it is for her. I give her a nod.

"We will find a bathing place once the storm passes," I add.

After the heat of travel and then the fear of the meteorite shower, a bath sounds nice, and I know Penelope likes them.

"That would be wonderful," she agrees, smiling at me.

I smile back, a little surprised at her response, though I am pleased by it. It is a nice change. She seems warmed by the way I take control, even though it is at odds with her independent instincts. Perhaps she has also softened towards me because I have not pushed for mating? I cannot say for certain. But no matter the reason, I will continue to treat her without that pressure, just as I promised myself I would.

However, keeping my distance from her has not become any easier. In fact, it is getting more difficult the longer I spend alone in her company, caring for her. Learning more about her. Still, I know I will manage it all the same. My patience will see me through. I continue chatting with her as I set up my own sleeping area, a respectable distance away.

She seems to love what she calls "pop culture," which I realize is short for popular culture. Interesting idea. I thought culture simply...was.

"...and one of my favorite shows is called *Black Mirror*. It's so good! I started watching it and then couldn't stop. Even though they're not exactly upbeat episodes, generally speaking."

I know at this point that a show is like a movie and both are stories told with moving pictures.

"You enjoy it even though they make you...sad?" I ask, trying to understand.

She laughs at my perplexed expression.

"I guess. Though maybe sad isn't the word...unsettled maybe? But yes, I still enjoy them because they're just so clever, you know?"

I must not look like I do, because she immediately launches into a detailed explanation of one of the episodes.

"I'll tell you about one that doesn't end too badly," she starts.

She lays out the story of a petty man who reproduces those who have wronged him in a fake reality based on another fictional show so that he can exact his revenge and feel like a king. I am glad the main female discovers a way to end their torture, especially when the villain reproduces a child.

"It is clever," I agree. "Though I do not know if I would enjoy anything but the end of it," I add honestly.

"Understandable," she acknowledges with a smile that slowly fades. "It isn't for everyone."

Again, I can hear the longing in her tone for all that is lost. It tugs at my heart. She herself feels lost, is clearly struggling simply to function, to find her role here in her new reality. This is why she has been attempting to be a co-leader in a terrain she is not capable of handling alone.

I can certainly relate to feeling lost. The Devastation changed our entire way of life. I can see why she is having a difficult time as she attempts to fit in here. The idea of helplessness, the sense of dependency it creates, is completely at odds with her deep need for self-sufficiency.

Although everything familiar to her is gone, I feel like she has spent much of her life filling a hole inside herself with activity, long before she ever crashed here. I do not know the origin of that emptiness, but it must have been something traumatic. Something that must be addressed so she can be free of it. I worry at that thought as our talk finally slows, pauses increasing. When she yawns, I tell her to lie down.

"We will be traveling again tomorrow," I remind her. "You need your rest."

She nods, lying down without an argument, the air between us far more peaceful than it was in the city before we left. I think I am starting to understand her better.

I move over to lie down on my own pallet, closer to the edge of the cave so I am between Penelope and any potential danger.

I keep watch for a bit, but the night is quiet, and tomorrow will be difficult enough without some sleep. So I finally lie down and close my eyes as well. Unfortunately, that is a mistake.

My eyes snap open at an unusual noise, a snuffling of some kind from inside the cave. Penelope lets out a yelp just as I jump to my feet and turn towards the sounds. It is a vregvan, one of small, leathery creatures that often live in caves. And it is going through our food satchels!

Cursing, I run towards it. It sees me coming and runs away quickly, its pointy nose twitching, mouth full of meat. I attempt to grab it, but it is too fast, slipping between my legs and rushing out into the night. It is not worth following it.

"What was that?" Penelope asks, on her feet now as well.

"A vregvan," I say, crouching to take in the mess of the satchels.

"Looks like we've been looted while we slept," Penelope observes, sighing as she surveys the damage.

I nod as I go through the previously full bags. There is barely anything left of our travel provisions—and we can't eat the food Rosalind sent for the New Village. Penelope comes to the same conclusion I do.

"We're going to have to hunt," she states, no question in her voice.

"Yes," I agree. "Hunting is now a requirement for the rest of the journey." It is likely to delay us significantly.

"You have to teach me how," Penelope orders, her tone already on the offensive. "I know I can help. I know there are some small creatures I can handle."

I sigh, rising from my crouch.

"Yes, there are small creatures. But they are no less deadly for their size," I retort.

I refuse to feed into her need to prove herself, especially when it would put her in jeopardy. I start to prepare to head outside as Penelope continues to argue with me. I refuse to engage with her on this. It is not negotiable. But then she says something that catches my attention.

"Is it because I'm a woman?" she demands, her chin raised proudly. "Is that why you won't teach me how to hunt?"

I growl. What a preposterous assumption! I give her a flat look as I lay out the facts.

"It is not because you are a woman—it is because you are human. Humans are soft. Even your men are unfit to hunt most of the creatures on Tajss."

Her cheeks flush and her jaw clenches. The mutinous expression on her face tells me she doesn't like that reason.

"That is ridiculous. And on our world, many of the women are stronger than the men," she adds, righteous indignation in her tone.

"I do not doubt it, but it's irrelevant. This is not your

world; this is Tajss. Teaching you to hunt would put you in danger. I will not do that. And that is final."

She opens her mouth, but then closes it again, stepping back even as she retreats into herself, looking away. I sigh, softening despite myself. I do not like when she is angry with me. *She* is the danger for me. But...perhaps a small compromise will not hurt.

"I will offer you a compromise." She turns to look at me, her gaze wary. "I will teach you the basics *in theory*. Not on the sands. For your book." I gesture at it, resting on her pallet.

She does not look impressed with the compromise as she shrugs and looks away. But it is the best I can do.

"I will be back," I say when she does not fill the silence. I linger at the edge of the cave. "You will be safer here. Do not leave the enclosure."

She does not respond. I hesitate, but then finally step out. I do not like leaving her alone, but there is no alternative.

I will hurry.

CHAPTER SEVEN

PENELOPE

I sit down on my pallet and wait for Bashir to come back. Demoted to being the helpless one. Again. Feeling too restless to stay there, I jump to my feet and start pacing. I hate having to depend on Bashir like this. I hate feeling like I have to be taken care of, that I can't take care of myself. Though I really can't deny that reality at the moment, can I?

Oh, it stings.

Logically, I know forcing Bashir to take me with him would probably just slow him down, but when am I going to get a chance to learn how to hunt? Every time I ask any of them to teach me, I get turned down! How can I stop being helpless if nobody will teach me?

I hear an odd sound and turn towards it, my heart picking up the pace. Was that another weird animal? I freeze as I listen, but I don't hear anything again.

Moving back to the pallet, I sit down with my back to the wall, so I can see everything. Again, made acutely aware of just how vulnerable I am here and how much I hate it. I sigh, grabbing my book to make some notes. At least it gives me something to do while I wait, instead of driving myself crazy with every stray sound or working myself up even more. I don't know how long Bashir is gone, but it isn't as long as I might have predicted. He's good at this. He shows up with meat that's already ready to carve up, hauling it to the back of the enclosure as I scramble to my feet to follow him.

"That was fast," I remark.

He grunts, setting the meat down. I want to contribute in at least some way, and I don't want him to refuse my help again, so I grab the extra knife at his side and start cutting before he can stop me. I feel him hesitate, but he doesn't say anything as he uses his main blade to do the same. Maybe it's silly, but working side by side with him makes me feel a little better, like I've vindicated myself in some odd way.

We cook and eat the meat quickly, packing everything up directly afterwards.

The meteorite shower delayed our journey, as has the pilfering of our supplies, but the trip isn't so time sensitive that it should be that much of an issue.

"I know a place to bathe that is not far from here," Bashir remarks, finally breaking the silence. "We will go there before continuing on with our journey."

I nod. A bath sounds heavenly. I'll follow Bashir blindly if it means I'll get a bath at the end. When we leave our snug enclosure, the suns are again beating down onto the sand, the temperature already rising, but I'll take it over the meteorites any day.

I squint up at the sky to be sure I don't see signs of any more deadly, flaming rocks, but it is clear and blue. They've passed, at least for now.

We walk for a bit, but then Bashir stops to crouch and look at the ground. I look down as well to see what has caught his eye and realize it's one of the sites where an meteorite hit the sands. Frowning, I lean in. The heat of the meteorite created a sheet of clear glass, melting the sand. It's actually quite pretty.

I turn to say something to Bashir, but pause as he lowers his head, his eyes slipping closed. He stays that way for a moment, and then a bit longer. What is he doing?

Without warning, he raises his fist and brings it down in a powerful move to break the glass. The shattering crack of the blow makes me jump a little in response. I wince when I see the glass shards, but he doesn't appear to be harmed, and he gathers them up, wrapping them carefully in a smaller pack without explanation. All right then. Maybe I'll ask what that was about later, but right now all I can focus on is the promise of a bath.

I wipe my brow and follow Bashir again as he continues to lead us, confident in our direction. However, I soon find out that "close by" must mean something different for Bashir than it does for me. We walk for hours before I see the small oasis we must be aiming for, with what looks like another small enclosure built there to provide shade over the water. By this point, I'm covered in new sweat over old from the blistering hot sun. Just walking into the shade is a relief.

I'm holding up well enough for now not to need another dose of epis quite yet, but I know from the interviews I've done that we need to ration it with care—or it could mean death. Another lovely aspect of Tajss. Seems like everything here has the potential to kill me.

My eyes adjust to the dim interior slowly. When they finally do, the sight of the spring at the center almost makes me want to cry. Water has never looked so good. All I want to do is take off my sweaty clothes and jump right in.

I glance over at Bashir and bite my lip. I can't bring myself to ask him to wait outside for me to bathe. The heat is a lot for him too, and it feels beyond selfish to ask that of him. Maybe if he could just look away so I could get in first...

Before I can ask, he turns his back silently. Again, I'm reminded what a gentleman he is.

"Thank you," I murmur, undressing quickly.

I slip right into the water with a moan of pleasure, the shade of the enclosure keeping the spring noticeably cooler than the temperature outside. Oh, it feels so good to wash the sweat away!

Bashir waits until I'm fully in the water to turn around. He strips without any appearance of modesty. He seems like he has no qualms about stripping naked in front of me, though I do avert my eyes.

Well...I mostly avert my eyes. I admit I sneak a quick peek as he steps into the spring after me. The light is dim, but I can make out his impressive musculature. It's difficult to miss. He reminds me of one of those superheroes in the vintage movies about comic books. Like Thor or Captain America maybe, with the addition of his dragon qualities of course. He is a tower of strength from head to toe.

One with a soul I'm growing to admire more and more. Yes, some of what he says chafes, but there's a bone-deep honor to the man that just can't be denied. Just like now.

I can feel his arousal, catching a brief glimpse that confirms it as he settles into the water. That brief glimpse alone makes my breath catch. But he controls himself—much better than I do, to be honest. He doesn't stare at me or move closer. He remains a respectful distance away. Too respectful of a distance.

I didn't think he'd be able to sneak back under my skin once I set my mind to duty, but I feel my control slipping away as we both linger in the cool sanctuary of the pool. I find myself drifting closer to his warmth, despite knowing it isn't a smart idea. I really shouldn't open that door again. It's so difficult to close, but I can't seem to help myself.

I see his shoulders tense as he realizes I'm moving closer

deliberately, not just drifting. I can feel his hesitation as I near. I lick my lips, feeling a touch of nerves.

"Why haven't you taken a mate, Bashir?" I ask in a low tone, the intimacy of the place asking for hushed voices. It's a forward question and a leading one, one I wouldn't have had the gall to ask had we not been alone, cocooned in this dim place. He licks his lips as he turns slightly towards me.

"I can only mate the right woman," he answers, his tone also low. Slightly rough.

I feel the warmth inside me grow at the texture of it. How can I resist the sweetness of that response? He shifts a little, accidentally brushing my nipples with his arm beneath the water. A hiss of pleasure escapes me at the grazing touch. He stills again at the sound, his own breathing accelerating.

I shouldn't do this, but I know I'm going to anyway. Swallowing, I lean even closer until my chest brushes against him again.

His eyes search mine as he finally moves closer to me himself, close enough to kiss. My breasts flatten slightly against his hard chest as his muscled arms come up to wrap around me. Slow and careful, watching for any signs of retreat on my part even though I'm the one who instigated this.

When I don't shift back, don't shy away from his touch, he sighs, and closes the distance between our mouths. His lips are soft, gentle, almost reverent as he kisses me, explores me slowly, carefully, not pushing too hard. But even that gentle touch has me heating up, wanting more, wanting that tender mouth on even more sensitive places.

But he draws back before I want him to, his cheeks flushed as he searches my face, his eyes soft and hot.

"You are the sweetest fruit I have ever tasted, Penelope," he whispers, brushing my hair back from my face.

I feel myself blush at the compliment. I don't know why, but it makes me feel more vulnerable than the kiss.

He frowns.

"Why do you blush? Why do you fear your power as a woman?" His hand slides down to cover my lower abdomen, his hand easily spanning the space between my hipbones, reminding me just how big our size difference is even though I'm a tall woman. "It is woman who makes life possible," he murmurs, his gaze sincere.

Makes life possible? I have a flash of an image. Me, pregnant and barefoot. Shoved into the role of a breeder. The seductive mood dissolves instantly. That isn't me, but that's obviously what Bashir thinks of me. What he wants from a woman.

I slide out of his hold, giving him a gentle smile.

"I think I'm done bathing," I say politely as I turn and walk out of the water, trying not to think of the view I'm presenting him with. It's the best I can do. I have to distance myself from him. From his idea of what I should be.

CHAPTER EIGHT

BASHIR

I am at a loss as Penelope leaves my side and walks out of the spring, her feminine silhouette backlit by the light streaming through some of the cracks in the shelter. Another rush of heat flows through me.

She is not far from me physically, but the mental distance leaves a decided chill. I must have said something she did not like. Before I spoke, she was soft and pliant in my arms, wanted me as much as I wanted her. I am sure of it. But now...

The air between us is odd. More uncomfortable than two people who just touched so intimately should be.

"Is everything...fine?" I venture when she does not speak another word, continuing in utter silence while time drags its feet.

"Yes," she says briefly, in a too-neutral voice as she moves over to our travel bags.

I do not like this. The way she left the water, her demeanor now. Her inner warrior does not combat me as furiously as it did previously, but she is also much more silent than I like. Something is wrong; that is clear. She clearly does not want to speak of it, and I promised myself I would not push.

She takes out a small vial of oil and pours a bit of it into her hand. I have watched her hands hold a writing tool, a knife to chop vegetables, a water jug—but now I am mesmerized. My eyes follow her slim hands as she rubs the oil between them and smooths it into the skin of her long legs, leaving them gleaming.

My heart beating quickly, I turn fully away from temptation. I cannot watch her like this and remain distant, so I will not look. I will wait until she comes to me.

I take a deep breath. I may as well get out of the water too. The charm of a bath has gone.

I need to find my center again, find that calm, placid place where clarity lives. I need to connect with the spirit of Tajss. I sit at the edge of the pool and rest my hands beside me, touching the slick rocks that are at my sides, in front of me, behind me, and under me, all the way down to the heat at the heart of Tajss. I can hear Penelope settling as well, the pages of her book rustling as I let my eyes slip closed.

I allow everything around me to drift away as I listen to the beat of my own heart, slowed now as I sink into the ritual of meditation. It is more difficult with Penelope there, so it takes more time than it usually does. But I manage. As my breathing slows, my focus switching to the internal, to what cannot be seen, I feel the spirit within me reach out, sink down into the rock underneath me, through the anchor of my hands. Sink down and call to the wise, fiery spirit of the planet.

When I lost most of my memory, most of the experiences that made me who I was, defined my sense of identity, I began to reach out for something, anything to ground me. My instincts were still in place, but the Bijass ruled my life, leaving me nearly an animal with no true captain at the wheel. Life was without any purpose beyond survival. It was a hollow existence.

I don't know when I began to feel and know Tajss on a level beyond the visible. All I know is that I spent a significant amount of time reaching out for something more, my spirit crying out for something to hold on to. At some point...Tajss began to reach back. It was a slow process, one I did not recognize at first. I slowly realized what I was touching. What was touching me.

Not only that, but I found myself changing.

The meditation, the connection with Tajss, bolstered my instincts in an unfamiliar way. Sometimes, my dreams themselves would forewarn me of dangers to come. Other times, I would keenly sense the emotions of others, before there were any signs of them visible.

When I first realized what the sacred connection was, I never dreamed how much it could help me, help all of us living in community on the surface of Tajss.

First and foremost, it has enabled me to keep the Zmaj in our community from killing one another.

It has helped me heal them. It has helped me find those who have lost themselves. It has helped me teach them how to find the peace they crave—just like Tajss had to teach me. It has helped me harness the destructive force of their Bijass when they are struggling.

I will never stop being thankful for the gift of making peace. There has been too much blood soaking into the sands of Tajss already.

Today, I am practiced enough that I can reach that connection to Tajss much more easily. It feels as though the spirit recognizes me now when I reach out. This time is no exception. I let out my breath and allow my consciousness to descend into a space filled with a deep, abiding peace, acceptance, a sense of being grounded that I crave.

At this level, immersed as I am, the thrum of Tajss is a resounding, cosmic heartbeat, filled with secrets that have long been suppressed. Hidden away. The energy I feel has a distinctly feminine taste to it, reminiscent of the women lost to Tajss. Prime mother energy. Powerful and nurturing.

The first time I felt it, the sharp pain of loss stabbed through me. We had lost so much. But the pain drifted away, slipped through my fingers almost as soon as I felt it, the negative emotion softened by Tajss herself. Just like today. The energy encompasses me, hugs me close, lifts me up. I sigh, feeling restored as I drift in the power, my troubles melting away from me.

I sense Penelope as my consciousness slowly rises again, closer to the surface of my mind rather than deep within where I was. When I open my eyes, it is to find her curious green ones trained on me.

Curious...and confused. She tilts her head as she continues watching me but says nothing. As if her intuition says not to break the silence quite yet.

I hold her gaze for a long time, soaking in her presence and feeling more than usual, with the touch of Tajss still lingering inside me. The essence of her sharpens in my mind's eye. I see more, understand more.

I can feel that Penelope is between...herself. Between the shield and the heart, attempting an unnatural balancing act that leaves her unsure of herself. A state she dislikes. Strongly. Ah. I understand fighting with oneself.

Perhaps she could benefit from some meditation as well. I pat the rock surface next to me, a silent invitation for her to join me. She hesitates only a moment before taking a seat wordlessly. I reach for her hand and place it palm down on the cool rock.

She finally breaks the silence.

"What are we doing?" she whispers.

"Being still," I reply softly.

A pause.

"Why?"

"So we align with the correct direction, the least perilous path for us to reach the New Villagers."

She frowns.

"By touching the rock floor?" she asks, skepticism creeping into her tone.

"By connecting with the heart of Tajss," I correct her.

Her frown deepens.

"I don't understand," she admits, searching my face.

I nod. Why would she? I did not understand at first either, and this is my original home, where I was born, a place I am a natural part of. But she does not need those things for this to become her home as well.

"Be still," I tell her. "I will show you. Close your eyes..."

She does as I tell her, though I can see she does not believe she will find anything. That is fine. Belief is not a requirement. Tajss is not arrogant. She does not need show her power, it is a deep well that simply is.

I guide Penelope gently to help her reach that deep state of meditation. Help her sink deep, deep where Tajss's life force beats, a gentle, powerful force. We sit there for a long time, Penelope still and silent next to me. When I slowly bring us both back up, back to our conscious minds, she no longer appears skeptical. But I can also see she is still processing her experience, so I do not speak of it, allowing time to pass. We need the rest, and she needs to absorb what happened.

Hours after connecting with Tajss, I can see Penelope's mind still attempting to work out the encounter. I under-stand. The first time was a transformative experience for me too.

Leaving her to her silent contemplation, I step out of the enclosure to feel the air around us. It seems calm.

Crouching over the fire pit that others built here, I thread some of the meat we still have onto a small spit, listening as Penelope moves around me. There is enough fuel for a small fire nearby, so I pile it neatly and set it aflame.

"Do all Zmaj pray to Tajss?" she finally asks, breaking the silence around us.

It is my turn to frown.

"'Pray'?" I pause. "I do not understand this word."

I look to her for clarification.

"Oh. Um...for humans, we have systems of belief, of faith, that we call religion. Many of these religions involve praying or worshiping an entity greater than oneself. Often to make solemn requests or offer thanks."

Interesting. I shake my head.

"I do not pray to Tajss," I say, turning the meat as I think. "I...*connect* with her. And in doing so, I connect to my own roots. Which in turn connects me to everything around us," I explain, gesturing to our surroundings.

"Connect?" she repeats, drawing nearer.

I nod, considering how to explain.

"There is no life without connection," I finally say. "We are all independent in our interdependence. Do you see?"

She looks away, nodding slightly, but I can see something is wrong. Her next words confirm it.

"Sometimes, we're better off just being independent," she remarks.

Ah. Her pain is surfacing.

"I do not believe that is so," I counter gently. "To carry out duty and mission is honorable, but there is no fuel without rest and re-connection. We are all of a piece, all connected, woven together." I interlink my fingers to help illustrate my point. "The heart of Tajss is very different than what you have come to see on her surface."

Penelope appears uncertain, seemingly mystified by this turn of conversation. Shrugging, she does not push the dialogue any further.

I am at peace with this and hope she considers my words. We cannot make it on our own, we come together, joined by the Edicts for survival. To think otherwise on Tajss is dangerous.

When the meat is done, we eat quickly. Penelope guzzles water and readies herself to leave when we finish. I start to do the same, but I feel a disturbance grate against my senses. Not a good one. I rise to stop her short of the door out of the enclosure.

Penelope looks at me questioningly.

"Wait. There is someone passing." I take a deep breath, rolling my shoulders. "I feel ill-intention."

I brace myself for an argument, but Penelope surprises me. Giving me a probing look, she steps back from the door. Good. I will not have to split my focus if she cooperates.

I take my lochaber from the scabbard as the threat draws close. Penelope freezes next to me as she sees me do so, her eyes wide on the weapon. The tension rises as the sound of footsteps reaches us. Her eyes move to the door. The pulse in her neck beats rapidly. I want to reassure her, but I dare not make a sound. If we can hear them, they may be able to hear us.

I will not let harm come to Penelope. My hand tightens on the hilt of the lochaber as I prepare to fight.

But then a distant voice calls out to the stranger, a muffled question I cannot understand. The footsteps pause.

Leave.

That moment of silence stretches as Penelope and I both hold our breath.

The footsteps start again, moving in a different direction, away from us. I do not release my weapon for a long moment, listening intently. I do not relax until I can no longer hear any sounds made by the interlopers. Letting out my breath, I put the weapon away. I will not have to fight at this moment, thanks to my connection to Tajss.

When I turn to Penelope, she is trembling. Triggered at the prospect of another abduction? I step closer, not wanting to cross any boundaries she does not want me to cross but wanting to comfort her.

"I will not let harm come to you," I reassure her, ducking my head to meet her eyes. "This I promise."

She makes a harsh sound. Does she want me to back—

She lurches forward, and her arms wrap around me, the desperation in her grip stinging me as I hold her close, make an attempt to help her feel safe. I do not want her to ever experience the acrid taste of fear, but I also acknowledge that this will not be the last time. Not in this world where we live.

She pulls back after a moment, a small span of time in which I can feel her draw the edges of tattered self together, regain her composure. She is strong, for all her outward softness.

"What do we do?" she asks anxiously, her eyes slipping to the door. It is no real protection from anyone. She realizes that, and it scares her.

"We wait," I say firmly. If I were alone, I might have attempted to slip out from under their noses. But I need to be more careful with Penelope. "There is food, water, and good company," I add with what I hope is a bolstering smile.

She returns it with one that trembles at the edges but does not crack. Brave. I feel a rush of tenderness for this scarred woman who refuses to break. I will keep her safe. Even at the cost of my own life.

CHAPTER NINE

PENELOPE

*B*ashir sits at the edge of the pool again, carefully taking out the bundle containing the meteorite glass he gathered earlier. I find myself drawn to him despite myself, despite my renewed determination to stay away. I can't help watching him, admiring his confident movements as he removes the sharp glass from its wrappings. He's being cautious, but it shows in his focus, in the rhythm of his motions. No matter how often I tell myself, "No!" and drag my attention to something else, my eyes sneak back to him.

Is Bashir my kryptonite? I sure don't feel like Superman. But I sure am starting to feel more and more like he might be my own personal weakness. Especially now. It's like that touch of danger stripped me of the growing wall I'd started to rebuild between us.

The determination in his face when those strangers were near made me know, beyond any doubt—he'll do anything to keep me safe. That counts more than his handsome face and beautiful body in the end.

I'm safe. It hits me on a level I don't have much defense

against. I've never felt like this with another person, like I can trust him with...me.

I sit on the ground next to Bashir, the sparkling water so beautiful in front of us.

He glances over at me, a touch of surprise in his expression at finding me so close of my own volition.

"What are you doing?" I ask, curious.

"I am preparing to connect to the heart of Tajss about the storm," he explains, unwrapping the bundle. "While we give trouble time to travel far from our path," he adds.

I nod, rubbing my palms on my thighs.

Am I going to do this? All the reasons why I shouldn't float through my head for the millionth time. They're easily eclipsed by my desire to be closer to Bashir, closer to the man I'm growing to admire more and more the longer we spend together. Maybe if we weren't forced to hole up in this private, intimate space again. Maybe if Bashir hadn't comforted me when I needed it. But those things did happen, highlighting the attraction between us, circumstances conspiring so I can't push it aside anymore. I'm tired of fighting this attraction.

Bashir is still watching me, a questioning look on his face at my proximity. I look at him squarely in the eye. I've made my decision, and I'm not afraid of going after what I want.

"Why don't you connect with the heart of me?" I murmur.

Brazen, yes, but I don't want to tiptoe around what I want now that I've accepted it. I don't want to waste any more time.

Bashir doesn't seem to mind my approach. His eyes flare with heat as he slowly sets the bundle aside, and reaches out to pull me closer.

I make a small sound as he sets his mouth on mine, his kiss hungry.

Yes.

I want this.

I want more. I wrap my arms around his neck, his arms encircling my waist, the strength in them making me feel ultra-feminine as his tongue flirts with mine.

There's no holding back my own response as my heart pounds, my legs squeeze together. My heated response only drives his higher, our passion mingling to create a combustible mixture I revel in.

Bashir is extraordinary in every way.

The attraction between us is undeniable, a force that can't be ignored, that I no longer want to ignore. I've been holding him at bay, keeping my guard up. I don't see the point in doing that now. Not anymore.

Why reject a man who cares, a protector who is truly invested in who I am, in my safety? It seems beyond foolish.

Perhaps I feel like this only because the stranger outside triggered those unwelcome memories. Brought my abduction right back up into my conscious mind, rather than the murky depths where I tried to keep it hidden away, even from myself. Even if that is true...I find I don't care. It simply doesn't matter, not with this tidal wave of passion that hits both of us upon contact.

Even the parts of me still rebelling can't make a dent in it, not through the fevered rush that encompasses us now.

There is no going back.

I give in to him with a purpose, shoving at my own clothes, releasing the curves of my breasts, exposing myself to him with intent this time.

I want him to touch me, touch me everywhere.

The pale pink tips are already hard, drawn into tight points as Bashir looks down at them, his hand cupping first one, and then the other, his touch just a little rough.

His control is as frayed as my own.

I sigh as he lowers his head to take one sensitive point into his mouth, my hands grasping his horns, caressing them.

He growls, the vibration sending a shudder through me, my center clenching with arousal. This is so much more than I could have imagined. So much hotter, so much more intense than I thought it would be.

He's always so in control, always so calm. Not now. He's letting himself go.

And my response to him matches. Because I want him not just with my body, but with all of me.

I ache for him to be inside me.

As if he can hear that thought, he picks me up, his face nuzzling against mine as he takes us over to the softest travel bag, laying me down on top of it with care. His cheeks are flushed, his eyes devouring me as he slides his hands down my body. I arch into the touch.

It feels good to be so wanted.

Gripping my thighs, he gently parts my legs, pushing them wide.

Then he stops just to stare. Savoring the sight of me spread in front of him. The ache deepens, creeping towards a maddening intensity. I bite my lip as he looks his fill.

"You are so beautiful, Penelope," he murmurs, the ache in his own voice daring me not to believe him. His eyes meet mine, the look in them both hopeful and...waiting. "Are you *my* treasure?"

My first instinct is to deflect the question, avoid the question and the reason behind it.

But...

He asks the question as though he won't keep going, won't proceed until he knows that I'm giving myself to him fully, that I want more than just this physical passion, just his body.

I reach out to pull him to me. He lets me bring him closer, but that's it.

His erection is impossibly large, a bead of pre-cum already forming at the tip. He wants to go further, wants this just as much as I do. But his determination to get a clear answer from me is stronger than his physical desire. He won't budge until he gets some sort of commitment from me.

"Are you mine?" he asks again, the eye contact intense, his hard length butting up against where I want him.

It's driving me crazy!

"Bashir," I moan, pushing against him.

"Give yourself to me, Penelope," he growls, his hand clenching on my hip. He's clenching his jaw, fighting himself not to give me what I want.

What we both want.

But he's still forcing me to decide. And I realize...there really isn't a decision to make in that moment.

Rising up on my arms, I kiss him, hot and clinging, my desperation to have him clear. I don't try to hide it. He deserves the same honesty he gives me.

I break the kiss, moving back just far enough so I can speak. My lips brush up against his as I do.

"I give myself to you, Bashir," I whisper, his eyes so close to mine I could count every long lash. "I give myself."

I barely have the last word out before his mouth is back on mine, before he reaches between us to take ahold of himself and push against me, come in where I want him to be so badly. I moan into his mouth as he enters me, stretching me wide around his girth.

The fit is tight.

He goes slowly and gently at first, letting me adjust to his impressive size. It takes some time. I slowly relax around him, my hands gripping his skin as I breathe deeply. The slow-and-gentle doesn't last long, not once my body gives way to his.

His rhythm turns less smooth, less perfect as he rises onto his arms, his hot eyes raking my length, devouring me. He's hot, almost feral as his animalistic nature rises from his core.

I shiver at the hint of danger, his hips pushing hard against me, filling me so completely I feel owned in the best way possible. His big hands knead my breasts, slide down my legs, cup my hips with a strength just this side of bruising, his exploration of me turning feverish.

I meet him touch for touch. My breath comes in gasps as I trail my fingertips along the ridges of his wings, watching as his eyes cloud even further from the intimate touch. I smooth my hands over his hard chest, his arms, the muscled length of his stomach. Every inch of him is perfect.

My eyes slip close as the pleasure overwhelms me, claiming my awareness of our surroundings. I'm not thinking of anything but him, of how he's making me feel. I'm falling, plunging deeper into myself, further than I've ever explored. There's a little fear there, but not enough to hold back.

I cry out as my body clenches with my release, waves of thought-erasing pleasure embracing me as Bashir groans above me, his grip tightening as he follows before I'm finished, my body milking his length.

I feel both lost and found as we merge, our bodies meshing even as our spirits touch in a blissful union.

This is more than sex.

More than a physical act.

If it wasn't Bashir, I may have been more frightened.

But it is him.

And I trust him.

I drift back to myself slowly, breathing hard, sweating. Bashir pulls out gently and lies down next to me, pulling me close, holding me tightly. I cuddle into his body as the sweat slowly cools on our skin.

Wow.

I lay my hand over the steady beat of his heart, rising onto an elbow to look at his face. He looks a little tense, his gaze unfocused as he thinks. When he looks over at me, I see a hint of fear in his eyes. A small, clinging fear. And I know why.

After what just happened, I also know why he pushed so hard for commitment. He's afraid that he's given himself fully and that I have not.

Feeling my heart clench, I lean down to kiss him tenderly, rubbing my lips against him as I pet his chest in soothing strokes.

I can't promise to understand his ways, but I'm willing to try. I can give him that. I can give my honest, willing desire to be his companion.

To...love him.

Even just thinking the word makes me anxious, makes me feel like I'm not in control. But that ship has already sailed. I can't help what I already feel. Bashir broke through my defenses long before this, and no amount of trying to push him out has worked.

Subconsciously, I tried to annoy him into letting go of me, something I can see now looking back. Whatever it is in him that staked that claim on me can't be budged with any strength of opposition I can muster. Or be blocked by my usual walls.

The idea of opening myself up fully to anyone terrifies me. I'm unfamiliar with the deep levels of trust that it requires.

With Bashir...it isn't as scary as it once seemed. He's not

my father. He's as different as a man can be. And our relationship is completely different as well.

With my parents, it was my mother who was devoted,
who harbored the undying, unconditional love for my father.
It caused her own sense of self to wither away to nothing in
the end when he so callously left her.

This...what I have with Bashir...is completely different. I
would be a fool to leave it unexplored because of problems
that have nothing to do with him. The truth is, I find I don't
even have the ability to deny him, not any more. I can't fight
myself forever.

I settle down next to Bashir again, my head cushioned on
his shoulder. It feels like a new beginning. A good one.

We stay there for a bit longer, cuddled together, enjoying
the closeness. But we can't stay there forever. Bashir finally
judges it's likely safe to leave, though I can see his own desire
to stay as well.

Responsibility really is a bitch sometimes.

As soon as we are outside again, I feel like we are on a
completely different journey than we were before the time
spent in the spring. I don't feel that same tension between us,
the emotions that had me snapping at him and perhaps
making rash decisions simply to make a point that doesn't
really matter.

When he takes the lead this time, I have no problem with
it. He's right. He's more experienced here on Tajss and better
able to lead the way. Now that I'm thinking with a clear head
instead of defensively, I can see that more easily. However,
we don't go far before Bashir stops abruptly.

"What is it?" I whisper, glancing around, trying to find
what has him reacting.

I don't see anything, but the land isn't completely flat
here. There are places to hide.

"We should go this way," he explains, his eyes opening.

"We may encounter those we heard earlier in the other direction."

I look the way we had been going, frowning.

"Are you certain?" I ask. "It will add more time and distance to correct ourselves later..."

"I have not severed the connection to Tajss," he explains. "If I listen, I can hear the danger. I am certain."

I hesitate, but then nod, following the new path with him. I don't know what I felt when he had me connect to Tajss, but I certainly felt...something. Enough not to dismiss what he's telling me now. Better to be cautious then regret it later.

We continue like this, adjusting the course when Bashir deems it necessary. At another point, Bashir steers us away from a sand dune in our path.

"Ioza," he explains. "The orange of the flowers is visible from here. Their spores induce euphoria and encourage sleep, so the vines may drain the blood from your body."

I blink at him. Then look back at the vines I can now see, interspersed with those orange flowers. Well, okay then. I'm totally on board with steering away from that direction.

We keep moving, making good time despite the necessary detours. I wipe my brow, my muscles burning from the continuous exercise, trying not to let the grueling travel get to me. To distract myself, I ponder on finding a safe way to harvest Ioza spores. The medical uses would be—

Bashir spins over to me and grabs me by the waist, his hard arm tight around me as he leaps into the air. My stomach drops as I latch onto him, my heart giving a hard thump, his flapping wings keeping us up in the air.

I open my mouth to ask what is going on, but then spot the reason. A large, lizard like creature crests the nearby dune, the humps on its back sporting vicious spikes. From what I can see of its teeth, they aren't much friendlier looking.

"Guster," Bashir mutters in a low voice. "Stay quiet."

He doesn't have to tell me twice. It moves quickly on its four sturdy legs, the webbed feet helping it glide across the sand, its sinuous movements silent as it passes by our laden cart, full of travel bags.

I watch with bated breath as it circles the cart, its leathery skin obviously tough even from this distance. Will it be drawn to the food? Was it packed tightly enough?

I let out a sigh of relief. It doesn't linger when it doesn't find prey. I watch as it disappears over the next rise. All told, the encounter lasts just seconds—only because Bashir was able to take us out of danger with his leap.

We hit the ground—the Zmaj aren't meant to fly, simply glide—as soon as the animal is out of sight.

"We must move quickly. It could decide to turn around and explore further," Bashir says in a low voice, taking hold of the cart again.

I nod. We push harder after that and it takes me a bit of time to stop looking over my shoulder for that leathery skin and sinuous movement. The suns are unrelenting, and the increased pace tires me even more.

When we finally do stop, it's beneath a massive tree, the trunk many feet wide, the tapered top of it sporting lush palm-like leaves.

"We will rest under the baoba," Bashir says, taking a critical scan of my state. "It is perhaps time to have some epis," he urges gently.

I take a deep breath, fully feeling the exhaustion, the unrelenting heat of this place. He's right. It's time to have some. I sit down and take out the supply I have with me. It isn't as fresh as it could be, but I feel the coolness traveling through me just the same as I chew on it carefully.

As I recover, I watch Bashir secure the area, ensuring there is no danger nearby.

It's the strangest thing. I'm likely on the most dangerous planet in the galaxy, but I somehow feel safer than I've ever felt. And I know it's because of Bashir.

How blind was I before to resist a gift like this?

CHAPTER TEN

BASHIR

My continued connection to Tajss means we arrive at the New Village safely, without having to fight the dangers we could have faced. I am thankful for it, but now we are entering a new kind of danger. Tajss cannot help me with it because we cannot avoid it.

The New Villagers gather around as we arrive, clearly leery of me. The looks they give Penelope are not much warmer. We stop just outside the village, people coming out to surround us as we do.

Most of the people are eyeing the cart while Jackson watches us, his face closed off.

"Why are you here?" he finally asks, crossing his arms as he surveys us.

"Rosalind sends her regards along with these food rations and supplies," Penelope responds, her hand indicating the cart.

Murmurs ripple through the crowd. The men and women look from Penelope to me, as if she cannot be trusted because we arrived together. I keep my face impassive though I feel the bitter bite of disappointment. I thought they would at least be more welcoming to her. Perhaps that was naive of me.

Jackson's eyes move to the cart. There is a minute change in his expression, but it is there and gone when he turns his attention back to me. There is refusal in his eyes. Will he really turn us away?

I look at the people who are still hanging back, spectators wondering how this confrontation will unfold. It is clear that they are hungry, that they are in need of the food and supplies we are offering. Will Jackson really be so petty as to turn us away when his people are in need?

"We should at least hear them out," Tessa, the brunette woman at Jackson's side, says quietly, glancing over at us. She says something else in a low voice, close enough to her leader's ear that I cannot quite make it out. Jackson's face tightens, but he nods.

"You may come in," he says gruffly. "Temporarily," he adds.

As if he has something to offer us we do not already have? I do not let the thought show on my face.

"Thank you," I say instead, echoing Penelope.

Perhaps it is not the best welcome we could have had, but it is still an invitation to enter. Penelope glances over at me and I nod. This might be more difficult than I first envisioned, but that only means we will have to be more clever in building our case.

We follow them into the village, knowing we have only been allowed in because of the cart full of supplies we brought with us. Rosalind was wise to send us with the gifts.

Once inside the square, Jackson barks out orders, and people hurry in to start unloading the cart.

"Where is Sarah?" Tessa asks as the activity goes on around us, her tone concerned. "How is she doing?"

"Sarah...she was really hurt. She had to be rushed to the city to save her life."

Gasps of dismay ripple through the crowd as they hear that news. But that shock is followed by some of those gathered looking thoughtful. I want to nudge those people.

"They were able to care for her at the medical center there, and now she is doing quite well. We saw her just before we left," I add deliberately.

It is good that they wonder what else they are missing by not allying with Rosalind. That they wonder what the city can provide for them that the New Village cannot. Pressure from the people themselves is a powerful force.

I can see that Jackson notices the realization of what the city has taking hold of his people.

And he does not like it.

He quickly moves on to a different subject in an attempt to take control of the conversation again.

"Obviously, Rosalind has an underlying motive for sending you here. So—what is it?" he asks harshly. A clear attempt to bolster the villagers' wariness of us and what we have to offer.

"She wants to be sure you are well," Penelope responds carefully. "That's why she sent the food and supplies."

Jackson frowns.

"There is no such thing as a free gift. She must want something in return. What is it?" he pushes. "I will not let you stay under false pretenses."

I lay a hand on Penelope's arm to stay her response. I see more than one pair of eyes notice the gesture, but I will not pretend to be so distant from her even for the sake of the mission.

I meet Jackson's eyes calmly, considering my approach. We cannot meet emotion with emotion. That will only escalate the situation when we need to do the opposite. We need to approach this with calm and level heads.

"We must all work together to survive," I say after organizing my thoughts, looking around at all gathered. Not just Jackson. They are all thinking beings. It is not only their leader I must convince. "It is Rosalind's hope that we can cooperate to that end."

Murmurs grow louder, the gathered crowd reacting to this announcement. It does not sound completely negative. Jackson hears this, but his expression remains suspicious, as do his words.

"We don't want to be under anyone's thumb," he responds with a slight sneer. "You may rest here for a few days. But then we'd like you to go back and tell her our response. We're not making any deals with a *tyrant*." He spits out that last word with clear disdain.

Penelope balls her fists, ready to defend Rosalind's honor. She admires the human woman greatly, but this is not the time to antagonize these people. I take her hand in mine. There is anger in her eyes as she turns the glare in my direction. I shake my head at her slightly. I can see her need to throw caution out, to do what she feels is right, but she reluctantly subsides, looking away. I admire her control and give her hand a quick squeeze. This all flashes by in a moment.

"Of course," I respond to Jackson for us, nodding. "We thank you for your hospitality."

Jackson does not respond, simply nods at a waiting man who leads us over to a building some distance away from the crowd. The quarters he shows us are meager to say the least, but we thank the man politely. Penelope is only waiting to speak her mind until we are alone. The fire of her anger is only banked, not extinguished.

"You should have let me put Jackson in his place!" she

growls, hands again in tight fists as she paces the small confines of the room. "Rosalind is *far* from a tyrant! And what the hell does he think Gershom was?!" she rants, turning to me. "Are we going to pretend Jackson wasn't one of Gershom's unthinking followers? That idiotic hypocrite! If it wasn't for Rosalind, everyone here would be *dead*! That's not an opinion—it's a fact!"

I make agreeing sounds as she continues to unleash her anger. She needs to release it, so I allow her to do so, now that we are in private, and it cannot affect the negotiations.

"I'm right!" she bursts out, turning to me for confirmation, her face incandescent with her righteous anger.

"Of course," I agree.

She nods decisively and continues on with the rant. She *is* right. But we are on a diplomatic mission and being right is not the goal. It is crucial that we not alienate the very people we have come to convince to work with us. However, she is not ready to listen to that reasoning at this point, so I will wait until she has spent her anger and frustration. She has a right to that frustration.

It comes from the empathy that is a natural part of her large heart, something she has been careful to keep hidden and guarded until recently. I am glad she feels free to show me this side of her now, this facet she did not want to expose before.

As she continues, spending her emotions, I notice the position of the suns in the sky. It will be time to eat soon. I should go hunt down our meal.

"I need to go hunt," I inform Penelope, gathering my weapons.

She stops mid-tirade to frown at me, bracing her hands on her hips.

"We brought plenty of food," she counters. "Why do you have to go find more?"

I sigh. She is not going to like this.

"It is easy enough for me to hunt and leave the rations to the New Villagers as a show of courtesy, of our intent."

Penelope crosses her arms and shakes her head, though she does not argue. I can see she does not like it, but she will see the reason behind this decision soon enough. I do not make the mistake of saying that now, when she is not thinking as clearly.

I enjoy my head attached to my neck, after all.

"I will be back shortly," I reassure her as I leave.

These people cannot hunt for themselves, and they know it. They will have to accept Rosalind's offer of cooperation eventually simply to survive. There is no way around that fact. They simply need time to see that.

And they need to see what I can provide. There is no better way to do that than to feed ourselves while we are here, not depend on them or what we brought. I predict that they will invite us to stay longer as their food stores dwindle, in the hopes that I will gather more food for them.

For now, they need to cling to their illusions of control, but soon enough, they will be all too willing to relinquish the reins.

CHAPTER ELEVEN

PENELOPE

*A*fter I calm down, I realize that Bashir is right about not antagonizing Jackson and the others, even to defend Rosalind. I still have to bite my tongue quite a few times as we spend time around the New Village.

I leave our quarters by myself the next afternoon, figuring I might be able to do more good on my own without Bashir there to remind them that I'm with one of the dreaded Zmaj. After getting to know him like I have, the whole thing seems even more stupid. I don't know anyone kinder or more level-headed than he is.

As I make the walk to the well for water, I smile at the people I pass, trying to look friendly and inviting. I don't always get a return smile, but the few that I do get give me hope. Maybe everyone here isn't as opposed to us as I fear. Even a small crack in the general shunning is a good sign, right?

Right.

Near the well, a small group of people catches my eye. They're gathered around a beady-eyed little man, his balding scalp shining and red in the sunlight. I frown. Elmer? If I remember correctly, he was the tailor on the ship. Sounds pretty innocuous, but he was actually quite a nuisance. His favorite pastime seemed to be riling people up with harmful gossip whenever he had the chance. Some people are just not meant to be around others, as far as I'm concerned. What is he saying that has people gathered around him like that?

When I slow to listen, he turns those small, mean eyes over to me, glaring as I walk past the little knot of people to get to the well.

"...Gershom was a lying fiend who nearly killed us all. However, he had some points that we should consider..."

Some of the crowd turn to look at me as well, their gazes unfriendly.

"...we have to be smart, we have to be in control of our own fates moving forward..."

I frown as I catch snippets of what Elmer is saying. What is he doing? I slow down to catch more of his impassioned tirade, hearing internal alarm bells ringing as rhetoric that sounds eerily familiar hits me.

He's espousing some of the anti-Zmaj, human tradition-alist ideas that Gershom had made popular. Is he trying to carve out a new identity based on the previous leader's persona? How can he call him a lying fiend and then co-opt some of the man's ideas for himself?

My sense of unease grows as I listen. This sounds like the same kind of incendiary commentary that caused the trouble between us and the Zmaj before. Between us and ourselves, honestly. And I don't like it one bit.

I also don't like being watched like a hawk while I fetch water, those hate-filled eyes locked on me as though I'm invading his space.

"It's a public square, buddy," I mutter under my breath as I retrieve the water.

"He doesn't care," a woman scoffs next to me.

I look over at the voice. It's the first time anyone has actually spoken to me. I get the feeling that isn't a mistake. Most of the New Villagers seem to be bent on giving me the cold shoulder.

"Does he do this a lot?" I ask, trying to get a conversation going.

She glances over at the small crowd gathered and shrugs.

"More than he should."

"The problem is those idiots over there who keep listening to the shit he's spewing," the man next to her says. "I'm Alec by the way," he adds with a small smile. "Sorry your welcome was so..."

"Unwelcoming?" the woman finishes, making Alec grimace. "I'm Sabrina," she adds, nodding at me. "And Alec's right. Elmer hasn't changed much since the ship days. Still causing trouble for the sake of it."

"Hmm."

I glance over to see him still glaring at me, his eyes taking in the first people who've deigned to speak with me.

"Elmer! Aren't you supposed to be on guard duty?"

I look over to see Jackson entering the square, his stern glance causing the crowd around Elmer to stir uneasily.

"I think we should have a more democratic way of assigning roles," Elmer argues back.

"We all need to take a turn. That is democratic," Jackson returns. "Go do what you're supposed to be doing." He looks at the others gathered. "All of you."

The crowd breaks up, and I see the flash of rage on Elmer's face, controlled in the next instant.

He holds a short staring contest with Jackson, but eventually turns and obeys the order.

Well.

That's something to keep in mind, isn't it?

"Elmer is trying his luck," Sabrina mutters. "I'm surprised Jackson hasn't done more already."

Alec grunts his agreement before changing the subject now that the crowd is gone.

I chat for a bit before they have to leave, then walk back slowly, seeing if anyone else will make an overture.

They don't.

This is going to be a hard sell, but we knew that coming in. I need to be patient.

A couple of hours later, I make the trip to get water again, and along the way I run into Alec and another man he's with. We exchange pleasantries, but the whole time there's an odd itch between my shoulder blades. I finally look over my shoulder.

Elmer is watching me like a hawk again. What is he doing, following me around so he can keep up the glare?

"I have to go," the new man mutters.

When I look back at him, I realize he's watching Elmer. As he walks away quickly, Alec's mouth tightens.

"It's like he thinks he's the fucking neighborhood police," he says, glancing over at Elmer as well. "I'll see you around, Penelope."

I murmur my agreement, my thoughts putting together everything I've seen so far. I'm starting to wonder if the attitude most of the Villagers are showing towards us doesn't have a lot to do with Elmer. If he's constantly stirring up hate, seeding their minds with these kinds of views, no wonder many of them are keeping their distance, going out of their way to be cold to us.

It's like the ghost of Gershom is still haunting this place. Something to keep a wary eye on.

I wonder what Jackson thinks of this. If I were Jackson, I would be worried. Turns out, I get to hear about Jackson's thoughts from the man himself. Later that day, he invites us to eat with them.

People mill around the square as he smokes some of the week's supply of meat. Bashir is smooth, sliding into small talk with Jackson easily enough. He keeps the topics light, getting Jackson used to speaking to him.

I keep one ear on them as I scan the area, my eye finding a familiar bunching of people in the corner.

And what do you know! There's that shiny bald head right in the middle of that knot again. As if I've called out to him, those mud-brown eyes turn to glare at me. Then he starts making his way over. This should be interesting.

Jackson stops mid-sentence as Elmer deliberately plants his feet in front of us.

"Yes?" Jackson asks in a tight voice. He obviously isn't happy to see the man.

Elmer looks at the meat.

"We should smoke more of it," Elmer announces. "We're tired of not having enough to satisfy a child much less an adult," he says in a voice that carries.

The people milling around us hush. I know they're all listening.

Jackson's face flushes with anger, but he holds on to his control.

"We need to be careful how we ration our food, or we will run out faster," he says in tightly controlled voice. "We've been over this."

Elmer's eyes shift over to Bashir and then to me.

I can see him calculating his next move. Jackson's reasoning is too sound to attack directly.

"Why are they still here?" he asks instead. "Haven't they had enough time to rest?"

"Where do you think this food you're so anxious to have

came from?" Jackson retorts, taking a step towards the smaller man.

He finally backs off, though I can see he doesn't like being physically intimidated into it. With his small stature and less-than-sunny disposition, I have to assume it's happened multiple times.

"You're making a mistake," he mutters as he walks away, just loudly enough to make sure everyone hears him. What a prize.

Slowly, the conversations between everyone there start back up, and Elmer is again ensconced in what I'm starting to think of as his groupies. How many pissing contests does Jackson have to have with that little twerp? It doesn't bode well for the strength of his position here that Elmer feels confident enough to defy him so often. Not only defy him but come at him with the intent to make him look bad, in this case.

Jackson is silent for a bit after the confrontation, staring at the meat, but obviously thinking of something else.

I exchange a glance with Bashir.

"I have heard some...concerning talk around the village," Bashir broaches cautiously.

Jackson's jaw tightens and he looks up from the meat.

I can see him debating with himself whether or not to say anything, to address the elephant in the room. He finally decides to speak.

"Elmer is an extremist," he finally admits in a low voice. "And he's definitely channeling the wrong guy."

The guy he's referring to has to be Gershom. Bashir tries to draw him out more, but Jackson has said what he wants to say of the subject. I understand that. I'd have a hard time truly confiding in strangers as well. I glance over at Elmer. That's someone that requires monitoring.

After dinner, Bashir and I go back to our meager accommodations. Not that I'm complaining. Just being able to relax out of the sight of so many judgmental eyes is nice.

"There aren't that many people who are willing even to just talk to me," I admit glumly once we're alone. "I feel like a total pariah here. So much for my role on this mission."

Rosalind would be so disappointed. Bashir sighs.

"You are doing a good job," he counters quietly. "Do not take offense at how wary the New Villagers are around you —it is my fault. They realize there is something between us."

"I don't think that's all of it," I say, shaking my head.

Bashir shrugs.

"Even so." Pulling me into his arms, he gives me a warm hug. I snuggle in, enjoying the sturdy feel of his body. After a long moment where I just listen to his hearts beat, he stirs. "Come. Let us find comfort where we can."

Bashir encourages me, grabbing our supplies and padding the beds, pushing them together to make a bigger one. Setting our things to the side. Hanging up a cloth to add some more privacy at the open window. It isn't much, but it definitely helps make the place cozier.

When we finally lie down, Bashir spoons me from behind, the hard warmth of his body helping me relax. But then he trails soft kisses up the side of my neck, his hand sliding down my hip. And another, even harder part of him, pokes me at the small of my back.

I'm not nearly as relaxed anymore.

"Bashir..."

"Hmm?"

He continues kissing the sensitive skin of my neck.

"Bashir...I don't think we should...do anything while we're here." Damn it.

He pauses in his caresses. I half hope he argues against me. I bet if we keep going in this direction, we'd both be *really* relaxed. But instead, he sighs, gathering me close.

"You are correct. It would be smarter to wait," he agrees.

Damn. This is one time I wouldn't mind being wrong. It's no surprise that sleep doesn't come easily after that. I want to go on that wild ride again with him, want that connection, especially while we're here in the heart of what almost feels like enemy territory. And I know Bashir feels the same, the hard length of him nestled against my backside.

When I feel myself weaken, I try to think of what Rosalind would do in this situation. It doesn't help all that much. Not when I know she would never be in this situation to begin with. Needless to say, what follows is a very uncomfortable night of sleep.

It doesn't get much easier the next time we lie down either. It's more frustrating than before we were together. Now I know what I'm missing! We do manage to get through it. But when the day we're scheduled to leave finally approaches, I'm ready to jump Bashir the first moment we have real privacy.

However, that need is tempered by the very real disappointment I feel over the fact that we didn't make more progress while we were here. I guess Bashir wasn't right after all. They didn't go back on the initial time period for us to stay and rest.

We start to ready ourselves for the journey back, going out to the well one last time to fill our water bags, when a commotion draws our attention. Frowning, Bashir grabs my hand and leads the way through the crowd to the two in the center of the noise.

Unsurprisingly, it's Jackson and Elmer.

"...you want us to be crushed under Rosalind's authority! You do not have our best interests at heart at all!"

"How do you propose we feed all of these people?" Jackson roars back, his sweeping gesture taking in all that are gathered. "Sometimes survival takes the place of ideology, especially ideology that has no practical application!"

Elmer sneers at him.

"You are weak!"

"And you're an idiot!" Jackson counters. "Tell me—are you going to go out and hunt for our food yourself?"

On the heels of that scathing remark, Jackson finally sees us—and Bashir's prediction turns out to be true.

"Bashir, Penelope, I am glad to see you," he greets us, a determined set to his jaw. "I just wanted to tell you that you are welcome to stay as long as you would like. And I wanted to thank you again for ensuring our food stores are full," he announces.

Wow.

Bashir was spot on with his assessment, calling it the first night we were here. Jackson is clearly smart enough to realize the meat will run out soon enough.

Bashir has managed, at least partially, to gain the man's trust.

It's difficult not to trust Bashir. His calm, stable presence seems to have that effect on most people. I look over at Elmer, who is clearly seething with rage, two spots of color high on his cheeks, his eyes glittering with it. But this isn't his call to make.

"Thank you," I say, turning to Jackson with a smile.

"My thanks as well," Bashir agrees. "We would love to stay a bit longer."

My eye is drawn back over to Elmer when he turns around and pushes through the crowd. I have a bad feeling about the look in his eyes. Like he won't go down without a fight.

Jackson needs to be more cautious about him. He obviously has a contingent of followers and sympathizers, which means he has some degree of power even if he isn't in charge.

But there's so much going on, the thought gets pushed to the back of my mind as the day continues. Perhaps it's all in my head, but I feel like the villagers might be starting to warm up to me. The hopeful thought is confirmed when Sabrina finds me, trailing a group of women.

"Hi Penelope—we were wondering if you'd like to help us prepare dinner?"

I smile, feeling excitement surge.

"I'd love to," I agree, at the same time trying not to sound *too* eager. I don't want to alienate them. "Lead the way, ladies."

I follow them over to the food prep area, feeling included for the first time as they continue to banter with each other around me.

"Of course, I wouldn't throw Alec out of bed," one of the women says giggling.

"Wash out your mouth Cynthia—you know he has a thing for Sabrina!"

"He does not!" Sabrina shoots back, blushing.

That sets off a round of raucous laughter that has me grinning in response. The talk has the time passing fast. With so many hands on deck, we make quick work of the meal preparations.

"Why the big dinner?" I ask curiously as we're setting the food out.

It seems odd when we know how cautious Jackson is trying to be with the supplies. Sabrina shrugs.

"Jackson says he has an announcement to make. He seems excited about it—wanted to pull out all the available bells and whistles." Her eyes twinkle with amusement. "Maybe he's going to tell us he's made a fresh batch of Elmer's glue we can use to fix some things around here."

"Sabrina!" I gasp, even as I laugh at the bad joke.

"We can only hope," she responds, not at all repentant.

I shake my head at her but understand the sentiment.

That little man is bad news. Once we have everything out, the whole village descends, the mood festive, a happy buzz in the air as everyone starts to eat and chat.

I know big dinners like this are a rarity around here, and everyone is fully enjoying the treat. Halfway through the dinner, Jackson stands up and calls for attention. I look over at him, along with Bashir, curious as to what this announcement is going to be.

"Thank you," Jackson says, nodding at everyone. "And thank you to everyone who helped prepare this dinner—it's wonderful." Everyone claps and cheers, the women who were involved waving their hands, Sabrina doing an exaggerated princess wave with a cupped hand. Jackson grins, waiting for the noise to calm down. "I wanted a celebration for the announcement I'm going to make because I think it could lead to something great for all of us here." He leans forward, bracing his hands on the table in front of him, a smile flirting with his lips. "I want to announce that I plan to launch an investigation into the mines to find what ores are down there."

A ripple of reaction goes through the crowd. Followed by another burst of excitement as people start to talk over each other. I turn to Bashir, who doesn't look surprised at all. I can tell that he saw this coming too. It makes too much sense. A discovery of potential value would make Jackson more powerful as a leader in the group's eyes—if he manages to gain access to the ores sooner rather than later, that is.

I can't help but feel he's fighting a ticking clock here. Elmer is just waiting for his chance. And he plays dirty. Very dirty.

I bite my lip as the crowd around us celebrates the announcement, unable to shake my worry for Jackson, for the New Villagers. We won't be here forever. What will happen once we leave?

CHAPTER TWELVE

BASHIR

"The hantif isn't the tastiest of plants, but it carries many essential nutrients." I crouch near one of the waxy, deep blue plants that grow wild on their property. "And when it is boiled at high heat, it releases a liquid that is a sharp, purgative medicine. Should anyone in the village fall sick, this plant will help their bodies expel the toxins or poisons responsible for disrupting their system."

Jackson crouches next to me, watching as I harvest the plant. He no longer eyes me warily when I am this close, which is a good sign. He seems to trust me now. Or at least much more than he did at first. Even while still maintaining his general distrust for most Zmaj. That mindset will take time to adjust.

Even my accord with him has not come easily, despite bringing offerings to ease the way. Jackson is reasonable enough, now that I have broken through the initial barrier. Once he realized there was no true threat coming from me, his attitude began to soften.

He is a decent man. He is also, simply, a scared one. As I watch his smaller hands touch the plant, I find I can sympathize. If I were so soft, so easily broken, I would be frightened of Tajss too. It is a sensible response.

In a way, Jackson's overly careful approach mirrors the fear of the Bjass we struggle with as Zmaj. I hand the plant over to Jackson, and he takes it with thanks.

"I appreciate the help," he says, clearly grateful. "This is going to be really useful for us."

I nod, appreciating how difficult it was for Jackson to reach this point with me. Humility is often something that needs to be worked on, for Zmaj males and human alike, I've noticed.

"What are your plans for the village now?" I ask as we rise from our crouched positions.

Jackson's face lights up at the question.

"I'm hoping we make more useful discoveries in the mine. Once we have something to use, to trade with, it will help us prosper, help us fix this place up even more..."

I listen intently as we walk through the village, enjoying his excitement. It is good he feels this way. There is a hard road ahead for these people, and some optimism will do them good. I can sense the same excitement that infuses Jackson running throughout the village, the people abuzz with the prospect of exploring the mine. I sincerely hope the endeavor proves fruitful for their sake.

As we walk through the people going about their day, my eye falls on Penelope, her golden hair glowing brightly in the sun as she kneels in the space between two of the buildings, her gaze intent on something low to the ground. What under the twin suns is she doing?

"Excuse me," I murmur to Jackson, breaking off and heading over to her.

"What are you doing?" I ask as I near her position.

She glances up at me, her face tense.

"I think I found Sarah's kedi," she explains in a hushed tone.

I look over between the buildings, my eyes scanning the shadows more sharply. Ah. There, pressed up against the wall, two large, bright green eyes stare back at me warily. The small, compact body is covered in a red-tinted yellow fur complete with stripes for camouflage. Currently, the furred creature is still as it watches, almost flattened to the ground on all fours.

"Is it Picard?" Penelope asks.

"I believe so," I say, lowering myself next to her. "It certainly fits the description."

"She doesn't look like she has any intention of coming out to us," Penelope remarks wryly.

"It does appear wary. Perhaps some meat?" I wonder aloud, reaching into my pocket for some of the dried meat I still have on my person.

I pull it out, place it on my palm, and hold it out for the animal to see. It sniffs the air, its long tail swishing back and forth as it mewls, but it does not attempt to come any closer. We try for a bit longer, calling it out to us by name. I try to creep closer when that does not work, but it only backs away when I do, so I come to a stop again. Then someone walks by, and the kedi immediately darts away.

"Damn it," Penelope sighs.

"Do not worry," I soothe her. "The animal obviously considers this place home. We will see it again."

"I hope so," Penelope mutters, getting to her feet.

"You will see."

It does not take long for my prediction to come true. The next time we see the small furry creature, it is lurking around our quarters.

"Bashir," Penelope whispers to me as she crouches down once more. "Over there."

I follow her gesture to see the fuzzy head poking around the corner of the building, watching us with those expressive eyes. Penelope is much more relaxed this time as she attempts to draw it out, cooing to it in a soothing manner.

"Come on, Picard," she murmurs, crooning. "Sarah wants to see you again. You remember Sarah, don't you?"

The low register, the sweet tone of her voice, slowly work their magic on the animal. It starts to walk towards Penelope, its ears twitching, the small wings on its back opening and closing, still somewhat uncertain. But it's slowly, inexorably drawn to Penelope's softness.

I can certainly relate, though it takes a much more circuitous route than I would have. It does not approach directly, but rather circles Penelope, casting me a suspicious glance where I stand, a short distance away. It sniffs at her, drawing ever closer, until it finally stops in front of her, deliberately within reach.

"That's a good girl," Penelope croons softly, reaching out with care to pet the soft fur. When Picard does not object, she picks the creature up slowly, watchful for any sign of resistance. But Picard has clearly decided to allow her access now, lying comfortably in her arms. Penelope stands, a big smile on her face as she looks over at me.

I cannot help returning that joy. I can see how much of a triumph this is for her, not only for overcoming her own wariness of a strange creature, but also for fulfilling her promise to Sarah.

We keep the kedi near us, play with it a bit, but then Picard decides she has had enough and runs away again.

"Let her go," I say, touching Penelope's arm when she moves to follow. "She will be back. If you attempt to trap her, she will not trust you."

Penelope looks over at me with a glint in her eye.

"Is that the philosophy you've been using with me?" she

asks seriously, though the twinkle in her eye lets me know she is teasing.

I grin.

"It worked with you. I think it will work with Picard."

She laughs, shaking her head.

The next time, the kedi conveniently reappears at dinner, just in time to nip at the pieces of meat Penelope feeds her.

"Intelligent little beast," I murmur, amused.

"You think she likes me?" Penelope asks, smiling at Picard.

"I am certain you have won her good graces," I reassure her. "That she is eating from you is a good sign."

Penelope's affection for the animal is clearly growing as well. Eventually, Picard wanders away again to roam and we are left alone in front of the fire. That is not a creature that will ever be fully tame, I expect.

"The villagers seem reasonable for the most part," I comment, enjoying the feel of Penelope next to me in front of the flames.

But I do not hold her as I would like to. I do not want to be responsible for the erosion of the good will we have built here so far.

"Yes," Penelope agrees. "It's actually going better than I expected," she adds, a slight hint of surprise in her tone. "Though I worry about Elmer still."

I nod. There is reason to worry about the man.

"I wonder what changes will be coming to Tajss," I wonder idly. "With exploring the mine, multiple settlements..."

We are definitely on the path to a different future now that the humans are here.

"I completely understand Jackson's excitement for the mine," Penelope responds, meeting my eyes. "I also think the Zmaj should strongly consider redeveloping Tajss. I don't understand why there's this general agreement that it won't happen again. I know it's possible. If it can be done once, it can be done again."

"Hmm." I frown, not knowing how to answer that.

I feel a warning in my gut when I think of highly advanced technology ever gaining strength on Tajss again. Or of connecting to other governments or forming alliances with other planets should the humans find a solution to the broken comms, as I know Penelope and others hope to. We have seen what lies in that direction, and it is not good. It was what led to the Devastation in the first place. Luckily, I do not have to respond as the topic turns again, this time to Rosalind.

"I wonder how Rosalind will deal with the clash of egos," Penelope murmurs. "It's a difficult line to balance."

"I believe it will work out for the best," I respond, fully believing so. "These squabbles boil down to survival in the end. They will die down soon enough."

Penelope snorts.

"What is it?" I ask.

"Nothing," she says, shaking her head. "I'm just constantly amazed at your ability to seemingly relax on command. Especially out here, where nothing ever seems to work out for the best. So far, there have been hitches and near-fatal blows at almost every turn."

I sigh.

"Sometimes the reason for events is not clear until we look back."

She turns to face me again, clearly not willing to entertain that thought.

"I doubt Tajss is going to ease up on any of us, or that there is a 'purpose' to any of this madness."

It hurts to hear the hint of bitterness in her voice, though I understand why she would have this viewpoint, consid-ering how she ended up on Tajss and everything that has happened so far. But I don't want to argue with her about this. I can already see her irritation and frustration rising. She will see in time that some matters need to be weathered. There is no point in dwelling on the struggle that is life.

Attempting to prevent an argument, I pull her close and draw her into a kiss, savoring the feel of her soft lips against mine. She is a little stiff at first, but that makes the way she melts against me even sweeter. I pull back after she is well and truly relaxed against me, her expression soft.

"I would say *we* have worked out quite well," I murmur, enjoying having her so close. "Do not worry so much. I will let no harm come to you."

"That's...really sweet, Bashir," she says, smiling at me as she snuggles in close.

My heart fills with an aching tenderness at the trust she has come to have for me. The fact that she no longer feels the need to assert her strength humbles me. Her trust is a gift I will cherish and do everything in my power to never break. I will try to never disappoint her. I hold her close while we sleep that night, hoping I will be able to live up to that gift she has given me.

The village is aflutter the next day. It is the first day in the mines.

The mines themselves are almost impassible, the way collapsed and narrow, so Jackson does not actually make it very far.

But he is able to tap into a vein he finds close to the entrance, coming back to the village with some pieces of ore in hand.

"There's a lot more where that came from," Jackson says with a happy grin, dirt smeared on his face. "Here—please take one for Penelope as a token of your time here."

I look down at the sparkling pieces, the glitter of them truly eye-catching. I shake my head.

"I appreciate the gesture, but I believe—"

"Please," he interrupts before I can fully refuse. "I insist."

I do not want to take what is theirs. But he is so insistent. Not wanting to offend, I carefully pick a medium-sized one in a rough oval shape. It is beautiful, with sparkles that catch the light with the many colors of the stars. Perhaps Penelope can fashion it into jewelry of some kind. When I find Penelope later on and give her the gift, her face brightens at the sight of it.

"Oh, it's gorgeous!" Penelope exclaims, taking the piece carefully, examining it closely. Rising up on her toes, she gives me a soft kiss. "Thank you, Bashir. This is so sweet of you."

It makes me want to shower her with gifts. I hear Tessa happily exclaim when Jackson awards one to her later as well. Perhaps it is a female propensity for shiny things? Whatever the reason, I decide I will be sure to bring Penelope whatever shiny object I find in the future.

Tessa hurries over to Penelope with her prize in hand.

"Oh, Penelope, look? Isn't it beautiful?"

The two crowd their heads together and marvel over their respective gifts. I smile, content to see that Penelope isn't being treated with distrust by her own people any more. No matter the harshness of the shell she erects around herself, her heart is tender. And she is eager to be of service, to help those around her.

I have been doing my best to counsel her on the group dynamics here in the village, confiding in her about my own struggles stemming from being out of touch with a good portion of my memories. But also letting her know that the roots of one's being are always there, always available to tap into, even if the experiences are out of reach. I am happy to see that the talk has inspired her not to worry about fitting into the group or building roots here. Her own spirit is the only root system that matters, and the more she taps into that sense of self, the less she needs to prove herself. A strong sense of self has a way of drawing people in, as evidenced by her inclusion into the group.

The longer we stay, the more we are integrated into everyday life. We help the New Villagers patch up some of the broken-down buildings, fixing windows, doors, walls. Many of the villagers have chosen to live together, but they will eventually want their own spaces, so more buildings need to be converted into habitable dwellings. I watch Penelope as we work, my chest warm with contentment at seeing her beam with happiness.

"Penelope—can you help with this door over here?" one of the women calls out.

"Be right there!" she calls back, wiping her brow and hurrying over.

She loves being productive, feeling like a part of the whole. We may as well make ourselves as useful as we can while we are here. I turn to continue lifting the section of wall up, my muscles straining at the weight.

As I do, my eyes fall on the little man with the beady eyes. Elmer. He watches Penelope, his eyes narrowed and unfriendly. It seems he is always there to watch us rather than do work of his own. My muscles burn as I heft the heavy piece up, looking away.

I am not concerned with him. It is clear the man is only looking for his moment to shine. Such vain reasons for aspiring to leadership never work out well, in my experience. Especially on a planet such as Tajss. A human as soft as he has no sway over this harsh world.

CHAPTER THIRTEEN

PENELOPE

"*A*re you having seconds?"

"No, I'm not—"

"I saw you circle through earlier! Don't tell me—"

"And you think I didn't see you sneak something in your pocket? Get real—"

I wince as an argument erupts between several of the New Villagers at breakfast—over rations. I understand the tension, but fighting about it isn't going to change the fact that soon there will be no food at all to bicker over. Reason is difficult to find when basic needs aren't being met.

Two of the men start posturing as they fight, getting right up into each other's faces. This could escalate into something physical very fast.

"I understand your concerns," Bashir cuts in, his voice pitched to carry even over the arguments.

My eyes turn to him along with everyone else's in the square. Bashir has a way to attract attention when he wants to, even though he's also able to somehow stay in the background at other times. Another useful skill. All eyes are on him when he has the fighters' attention, continuing as he moves closer. Ready to intervene with his body, if necessary.

Be careful, Bashir. I'm growing pretty attached to that body.

"You don't understand anything," someone mutters.

Bashir raises an eyebrow but doesn't respond directly to the comment.

"There is enough food for everyone. You should not focus on the lack." He looks around at those gathered. "I will hunt more meat before Penelope and I depart to replenish your stores."

That seems to break through where his other words didn't. The tension drops. The two men who were about to come to blows separate. Conversation starts up again. Just like that, the situation is deftly diffused. The way Bashir can handle people...it's truly amazing. But these problems aren't just going to go away. What are they going to do when Bashir and I leave?

After spending time here and seeing the day-to-day life, it's clear that they can't take care of themselves. It makes much more sense for them all to just go to the city. To make matters worse, everyone here isn't so sure about staying. I can see the longing in the eyes of plenty of the villagers when they're reminded of what the city has to offer them. Things they just don't have access to here, like enough food, health-care, and plain old physical security, just to name a few. It's truly ridiculous to stay.

I can understand the allure of "having their own place," but only if they can sustain that place. Otherwise it's just a place they've chosen to wither away in. That's exactly what I fear this is. They clearly cannot take care of themselves here, cannot meet everyone's most rudi-mentary needs. Still, both Jackson and Elmer seem intent on not budging from the directive to remain. It makes absolutely no practical sense and makes me doubt if *either* of them are a good choice for leading these people.

The mumbles and whispers that take over after the confrontation during the breakfast that Tessa went to great trouble to prepare don't sound all that optimistic. After all, I can't be the only one having these thoughts. The villagers themselves likely don't want to air their opinions around their dueling co-leaders.

I sigh, focusing on my own breakfast as I wonder about how everything will work out. And if it will be peaceable or painful. There's no telling at this point which way it'll go. At least the morning has returned to relative normality again.

I have that thought too soon. The conversations around me taper off until no one is talking. Is there another confrontation brewing already? I don't see anyone at each other's throats. And I don't hear any raised voices...

The New Villagers directly in front of me are all staring in the same direction. Some of them have their mouths hanging open. A small piece of meat falls out of Tessa's mouth, and she doesn't even notice. The people at other tables are staring in the same direction, too.

My eyes naturally find Bashir next, like I need to reassure myself with the sight of him. But his surprised expression doesn't calm me. It does the opposite.

My stomach clenches and my heart beat speeds up as I slowly turn in the direction everyone is focused on. I'm moving in slow motion. Like that point in a horror movie when you just know it's going to be something bad, but you have to look anyway.

"Oh...shit," I whisper under my breath, my eyes locking on the reason for the stunned silence.

It's a...creature for lack of a better word. A huge creature. Maybe "monster" would be an appropriate term to use here. It must weigh at least a couple of tons, covered in leathery gray skin except for a mane of white hair just under its massive head, like a collar around its thick neck. It walks on all fours, its feet a mix between paws and an almost birdlike foot, with long sharp claws. The head isn't quite lizard-like, the muzzle too short to qualify. The teeth that are revealed by its slightly open mouth must be razor sharp.

I have no idea what the hell that thing is. But I know by Bashir's reaction that it must be out of its natural habitat. Perhaps because of the storms, like the bird near the wall days ago?

I guess the reason why doesn't matter so much right at that moment as the thing heads directly for the food on the breakfast tables.

Bashir grabs his lochaber while we're all still staring in stunned silence. The roar he lets out snaps me out of my frozen state, while also drawing the thing's attention.

Be careful!

My heart is in my throat for a different reason now as every eye fixes on Bashir, where he comes to a standstill directly in front of the creature. His eyes meet the thing's pitch-black ones, his gaze strong and fearless. Time seems to freeze as we all take in the massive size difference between the creature and Bashir.

Bashir should look ridiculous as he stands in front of the thing with his weapon, but something about his face, his defiance in the face of all that power...

He doesn't look ridiculous at all. He looks fierce, like the warrior he is. His eyes dare the thing to try to go through him. His sudden appearance, combined with the loud war cry he uttered, even stops the creature. It looks unsure of itself for a moment, warring instincts telling it to both charge forward and to retreat. It likely isn't accustomed to other creatures showing no fear when faced with its massive size. Especially not one so small in comparison.

I hold my breath, wondering if this is all it will take to get rid of it. If it will turn around and leave the village now. But that's too much to ask for.

Its primary instincts click back into place, and it huffs out a harsh breath as it slinks forward again, powerful muscles moving smoothly under that hard-looking skin.

Bashir is ready for the movement. Darting to the side, he slices at the back of one thick front leg before sprinting to the other side and doing the same there. The creature obviously wasn't expecting that kind of attack, letting out a surprised shriek of its own as it falls to its knees in response.

But that doesn't mean it isn't dangerous still. I cry out as it snaps those powerful jaws at Bashir, quick as a snake despite its bulk. Bashir leaps out of the way in the nick of time, his wings flaring to help.

Unfortunately, the movement puts him directly in the way of the thing's thick tail. It knocks him out of the way, forcing Bashir to scramble to avoid the hind legs it then kicks out at him. There's no way a full hit from that thing won't do serious damage. I stand up, fear sinking its painful claws into me as Bashir pushes to his feet.

He's a vision of determination, a sheen of sweat covering his tense muscles. He has to steady himself from the blow, but it takes him less time than I would have expected. Less than two seconds after, he's moving just as quickly as before, swiping fast and hard to knock out the creature's hind legs. Already struggling from the slices to its front legs, the thing throws back its head to roar while it tries to get back up without any luck.

Bashir leaps onto its back and swings his blade high into the air, the sun glittering off the sharp edge, his wings spread wide for balance. It's a stunning sight. He brings the weapon down in a stabbing motion, the sharp tip plunging into the area just past the base of the thing's skull.

A moment of hushed silence all around. The head falls forward limply. And, just like that, it's dead. The ground trembles as its weight falls.

Bashir pulls his weapon out of the creature, the full length of the blade covered in dark blood as he stands on its back.

It's dead, but...there's something wrong with Bashir. I sprint forward before anyone else starts to move, my concern rising as I see how dazed he looks, his eyes clouded.

It's the Bijass.

The fight must have reignited his instinctual, animalistic side. I stop at the creature's side, hoping it is really dead. Pushing that thought aside, I look up at Bashir.

"Bashir," I call out softly, not wanting to startle him.

He slowly turns to look down at me, a glimmer of something appearing in his eyes.

"Bashir, come down," I try, adding a gesture for good measure. For a moment, I think I may not have gotten through to him. The Bijass can be all-encompassing. It's possible that—

He leaps down in one graceful movement, landing in a half-crouch right next to me. I let out a startled squeak but stifle it quickly. I don't want to rile him up.

"Come on, Bashir," I say in a calm, crooning voice, reaching out slowly to take his hand. He lets me even as his eyes drift over to the others watching. They narrow with suspicion. Uh oh. I need to get him away from all these people—right now.

"Bashir," I say a little more sharply. He looks back over at me. "Come on—we're going back to our quarters. Okay?"

As I talk, I start walking, tugging him along behind me. He follows easily enough, but every time I stop talking, his attention starts to wander. Dangerous. So I keep talking. I talk the whole way back, gesturing at everyone to get out of our way. I don't know what they'll do if he attacks. So I won't let him. The walk feels much longer than it is, my hold on Bashir's hand probably painfully tight though he doesn't react to it.

I breathe a sigh of relief when we finally make it back to our building and I close us inside alone, until I realize now I need to figure out a way to bring him back to himself.

I turn around to see Bashir watching me intently. It's really scary to look into his eyes and not see the same person looking back. I'm so used to his being the one in control, the one who is calm and reasonable. I'm going to have to be that person for him now. He needs me to be.

"Bashir," I murmur, walking over to him with controlled movements. "Bashir, come back to me."

I reach up to cup his face and something flickers in his eyes, but then drifts away again. Maybe if I touch him more? Sliding my fingers into his hair, I tug his head down far enough so I can place my lips against his. This has to work. I don't know what else to do. I've already talked his ear off. That didn't work to do anything but distract him.

His lips are still against mine, so I kiss him slowly, my arms wrapping around his neck as I stretch up against his hard body. I'm starting to wonder if I need to try something else when I feel his body start to respond. Then his lips start to move against mine. Oh, good—

I gasp as he suddenly picks me up with a growl and tosses me gently onto the bed.

"Bashir!"

He covers me in the next instant, his hips grinding against mine, his erection hard and pulsing even through our clothes —which don't last long. He yanks mine off before tearing off his own.

Then his sparkling eyes are looking down on me as he pushes my thighs open and takes hold of my knees, lifting them up and apart. I can't look away from those intense eyes as his erection nudges against me. I'm already so wet and ready that he starts to slide in at the touch, his girth stretching me. I moan as he fills me, slowly and relentlessly pushing his entire length inside me, his gaze on my face the entire time. Then he starts to move. Long, deep thrusts, his jaw tight, his grip almost bruising as my own fingers dig into the bed on either side of me.

I clench down on him as an orgasm hits me unexpectedly, my hands coming up to dig into his forearms. He brings my legs down so they're wrapped around his waist, leaning over me, his face still intent on mine. But his face is somehow softer now, his eyes clearer.

"Bashir?" I ask, my hands sliding up to grip his broad shoulders. I've never seen him give in to his Bijass. Can I even bring him back?

His gaze flickers, but he doesn't say anything, his rhythm increasing, the feel of him inside me making me arch up against him in response. I'm getting close again.

I prop myself on my elbows and kiss the side of Bashir's neck, rub my face against his damp skin.

"Come back to me, Bashir," I whisper into his ear. "I need you."

His body shudders against me.

"My treasure," he grates out of clenched teeth.

I fall back down, my heart clenching with joy.

"Yes," I agree, smiling up at him. "Yes, I'm your treasure."

His eyes clear in front of mine, his gaze sharpening. Reaching between us, he rubs at me where we're joined. In the next second, I'm coming again, my cry muffled by his mouth against mine, the kiss voracious, but tender in a way it wasn't while he was still not himself. With a moan of his own, he pushes deep inside me, bucking with his own release. I hold him as he trembles above me, so relieved I have to choke back some tears. Bashir is breathing deeply as he finally raises his head to look at me.

"I am sorry," he whispers, searching my face. "I could not hold on..."

"Shh." I kiss him softly, holding him tight. "It's okay."

We stay there like that, wrapped in each other for some time. Needing the comfort, the closeness. After hours alone, Bashir finally stirs, ready to face the village again. This time when we leave, I keep my hand firmly in his when he tries to tug it away. He looks over at me, a questioning look in his eyes.

"I don't care what they think about us being together. Let them deal with it," I growl.

A flash of surprise, then a warm smile as he tightens his grip on me. But, as it turns out, I'm the one surprised.

When we reach the square, most of the village is still outside. When they see him, they don't seem to care at all about what we were or weren't doing. They erupt into cheers!

"Way to kick ass, Bashir!"

"How the hell did you manage that?"

"That was amazing!"

Bashir looks as surprised as I do at the warm reception, then a little uncomfortable with the attention. He nods at everyone graciously, taking the pats on the back with a grain of salt as he leads the way over to the creature's body. It's still lying at the edge of the village, untouched.

"I will dress the chatteron," Bashir announces, duty steadying him, getting him back onto even ground. "Now there is extra meat, so no more arguing over rations," he adds, smiling.

Answering laughter erupts as he moves forward to deliver on that promise. It's taking him some effort to summon the energy to do so. The blows he took from the monster aren't all that's responsible for the heaviness of his trudging walk over to the carcass. There's a shift in him, the distance he adopts as he switches to auto-pilot. He should be sleeping, but he won't do that.

I suspect at least part of it is because he's ashamed he had such a difficult time reigning in the Bijass. Like he should be above it somehow. He'll keep going, keeping helping until we return to the Tribe.

I admire his selflessness. But that doesn't mean I don't worry. He isn't a superhero, and he shouldn't feel like he has to act like one. The sad part of it is that he has no reason to feel ashamed in the first place. He used that natural instinct his kind need on this planet to survive, and he saved all of our lives with it. Maybe he thinks of the Bijass as primitive or brutish, but he needs it to survive. Because we weaker humans depend on the Zmaj, we need it too.

Maybe it isn't perfect, but what is?

The New Villagers are of the same mindset, completely won over by Bashir's heroic act. It's stupid that they needed such a spectacle to see how worthy a person Bashir is, but I'm glad for their change of heart all the same.

I follow Bashir over to the beast and join in to help cut and process the meat from the creature that had ironically intended to have *us* for dinner.

"What did you call this thing again?" I ask, grimacing as I cut into its tough hide with a long knife.

I very consciously *don't* complain about the hours it will take to gather all of the meat from such a ridiculously big animal. If Bashir can kill it and then fight back the Bijass to find himself again, I can damn well help butcher the thing.

"Chatteron," he repeats, a frown marring his forehead.

"What's wrong?" I ask, seeing he's disturbed by something. He sighs, shaking his head.

"I'm concerned that the meteorite shower has disturbed

the creatures of Tajss," he admits, his tone and expression foreboding. "Chatterons...they should not be in this area. It is not the territory they normally roam."

He seems quite disturbed by the thought. I can see why. If there are more creatures like this wandering around now where they shouldn't be, well, that's terrifying.

"We have to get back to the tribe, back to Rosalind," Bashir continues. "Soon. We must ensure they are still faring well."

That isn't reassuring at all. I attack the chatteron with renewed vigor. If Bashir says soon, I'm sure he means the quicker, the better.

As Bashir cuts into the meat expertly and I hack at it attempting to emulate his technique, Jackson joins us, taking out his own knife.

Before he starts in on the creature, he raises the knife and turns to Bashir, obviously aware of the audience. He raises his voice to be heard.

"You are always welcome as an ambassador, Bashir. We are all in your debt."

The crowd cheers again, agreeing with that sentiment. Jackson smiles, pleased, but I feel uneasy still. This won't sit well with Elmer.

I don't dwell on thoughts of Elmer. Not when a much more savage threat looms. If they're stirring and leaving their natural habitats to wander in large numbers... This could be catastrophic.

CHAPTER FOURTEEN

BASHIR

I prepare another cut of meat for the smoker, slicing off a slab from the haunch of the giant carcass and then shaping and trimming it. The sheer amount of time it is taking to process the meat for the entire slain creature is both helping and hurting my state of mind. I feel better focusing on something that I can actually do. It must be done correctly, or the meat will spoil and be wasted. But the work itself is not so mentally consuming that other thoughts do not occasionally intrude, despite my intentions.

I sigh as I work, frowning. The shame I feel for having lost control of my Bijass is not something I can easily put aside, despite my desire to do so. Every time I am not completely focused on the task at hand, that self-loathing in the pit of my stomach grows and grows.

I do not know why something deep within me whispers to me that I have failed. Failed at controlling myself. Failed to be the kind of Zmaj I want to be. Perhaps it is some section of stored memory I have not yet been able to tap into. Some knowledge or experience I can no longer access, at least not with my conscious mind.

I do not know. All I know is that the emotion is draining me. Logically, I know that I require the Bijass at times. That it is likely the reason I am still alive today after everything that has occurred on Tajss. That is a necessary aspect of what and who I am.

Still, the fact that I could not control it is disturbing. It has never felt quite that strong, that all-encompassing, before. Not since I initially regained control of myself, fought back to the light, to myself. And I believe I know why that is the case.

I glance over at Penelope. She wipes her brow next to me, her gaze focused as she continues to help me, support me. When I think of the sheer terror I felt when I thought that creature might harm Penelope if I did not take care of it swiftly...

I stifle a growl even now, just from thinking of it. I look away from her, bring myself back to the present. I take a deep breath to dispel the memory, anchor myself. It is clear to me that I lost control because of that fear for her.

Simply thinking of the situation is enough to trigger a response even now, when I know she is safe. That aspect of it is something I can understand. Of course I would want my most primal self, my strongest self, to come to her rescue when needed. And it *was* needed. I do not think I could have destroyed the chatteron, at least not as swiftly, without it.

That is not what brings shame bubbling up from the depths. The problem is what happened after my foe had fallen. I stab into the meat with a little more force than necessary. I should have been able to rein myself back in. Should have been able to put my own beast back into the confines that I keep it in when it is not needed. I have always been able to keep it there whenever I desire, ever since I regained control. But I was not able to.

I take another deliberate deep breath, attempting to calm

myself as the trapped panic of that period tries to reassert itself. Even now, the shame makes me feel as though the villagers around us are judging me for my lack of control. Though they have even gone so far as to cheer for me when I returned from our quarters with my mind again my own.

"Bashir? Is everything okay?"

I look over at Penelope's concerned voice. Her cheeks are flushed from the sun and the exertion of our efforts, her eyes hint at the same worry that is clear in her voice. I am obviously not hiding my emotions as well as I think I am. I give her a reassuring smile that feels strained and does not seem to reassure her all that much.

"I am fine," I try, looking away again, not wanting her to see the lie in my eyes. Not wanting to spill all of what I am feeling. I feel her hesitate at the short response. But I clearly do not want to talk, so she accepts my answer, moving on with her work, though I feel the worry she harbors for me.

Now guilt adds itself to my already raw emotions. I do not want to rebuff her. I am behaving more distantly towards Penelope. And that is not right. All she has done is help me, been kind to me. Supported me, even now.

I need to manage my reaction better, need to find a way to let go of this shame that is eating at me from the inside. I throw myself back into the work, moving faster in an effort to focus all of my mind on the task. Perhaps if I fill myself with other thoughts, the negative ones will not have as much room to grow and fester. It does help to focus on the village's needs instead of my own internal dialogue. So that is what I do.

I work hard, finishing most of the cutting and smoking of the meat before it is time for a break. A break in which Jackson pulls me aside for help with further exploration deeper into the mine, where the trek is more perilous.

"...wouldn't it be better if we try to navigate without a

light source? It could draw anything living in there to us," Jackson says.

It is one of many not so practical ideas he has voiced in the last few minutes. I am starting to understand that logic is not always this human's strong suit.

"We need to be able to see in order to avoid danger. And perhaps accidentally cause a cave-in," I explain, holding on to my patience. "It would not be advisable to go in blind when it is not necessary."

I am trying to help him see his ideas in a more critical, more real-world light, according to what is sure to fail and what *might* work. Unfortunately, I am unsure whether Jackson is really listening to what I am saying. He seems quite set on his on viewpoints and opinions. When he waves away my comment and moves on to another idea, I fear I am correct in my impression. I sigh internally but keep my frustration to myself. Showing my anger now would be counterproductive to what we are here to accomplish. It would alienate Jackson when I need to befriend him.

This behavior is quite baffling. Human males may not have the Bijass, but there is something Penelope has told me is called "ego" which I think Jackson may be under the influence of. At least where his ideas are concerned. I gather this ego does not always fall into logical or reasonable lines.

The practical implication of that now is I feel somewhat exhausted after having the talk with him. By the time we are all done with dinner, I am ready to be alone with only Penelope by my side. Before we retreat to our quarters, however, we decide to take a detour to bathe first. The days are hot, leaving us coated in sweat and dust. Today we also have the blood of the dead animal on us, which most definitely needs to be washed off.

While we bathe, my eyes are inescapably drawn to the sight of Penelope's naked, wet skin. It has me itching to be alone with her. To touch her. To stroke every curve of that streamlined body.

By the time we do make it back to our quarters, I am hungry for her, my cock hard and throbbing for a taste. We walk into our private area, Penelope still speaking of...something. I try my best to listen to whatever she says, but I would be hard pressed to repeat the content of what she is currently saying.

"I don't think—"

"Come here," I murmur, interrupting her to wrap my arms around her waist and pull her close.

Her eyes widen as she feels my hard length against her belly, but the surprise quickly gives way to interest. And heat of her own. Heat that I am grateful to see.

I pick her up, and she wraps her long legs around my hips as I bring my mouth down to kiss her upturned, waiting lips. I moan at the taste of her, at the feel of her. Yes. This is what I need right now. The kiss is deep, hungry, small sounds escaping Penelope's mouth only to be swallowed by mine as I keep my lips pressed to hers.

I make my way over to our bed, laying her down onto it before stopping only briefly to divest us both of our clothes. Penelope beckons me back with hungry eyes, sitting up to pull me down to her. I do not think I have ever seen a more welcome sight.

Groaning, I let myself be pulled down and set my mouth back on hers as she reaches for my erection, aiming it at her ready entrance. I gasp as I feel the hot wetness there. All for me.

I push forward as she thrusts her hips up to take me in, both of us working to get me in as deep as I can go. With no more restrictions around the New Villagers, Penelope is free and as eager as I am, merging with me with abandon. As I meet her kiss for kiss, thrust for thrust, she is almost insatiable, possessed with desire. Desire for me. It only heats my blood more.

Matching her fervor with my own, while being careful to hold back the full depth of my passions so as not to crush her under them, we make love as if nothing else matters, as if we are the only two who exist. I touch the hard tips of her breasts, the soft skin on the insides of her thighs. The firm little nub at the apex of her sex that makes her cry out with pleasure. I grit my teeth as she squeezes down on me.

To my surprise and pleasure, once is not enough for her that night.

"More," she mutters, pulling me back in for another kiss, her face flushed, breasts pink from the attention I have already showered on them. I give her what she desires. It is no hardship.

I marvel at what has gotten into her after we make love twice more during the night before she is spent, but I do not question the gift. She is a sure treasure. I thank Tajss for such an extraordinary woman every day. It took time, effort, and patience to circumvent her defenses, to show her she could trust me. It was worth it. I would do it all again and more to win her.

Satiated physically, my heart contented, I finally fall asleep with Penelope held close in my arms. Unfortunately, I do not sleep for long. A harsh banging wakes both of us up, pulling us out of our sound sleep.

"What is it?" Penelope asks, her eyes clearing rapidly. "What's that sound?"

"Meteorites," I mutter, hearts racing as I slide out of bed quickly. "Stay here," I tell her.

I rush to the door, hoping I am not too late. When I pull it open, one of the flaming rocks crashes only feet away from me, sand bursting into the air and pelting my feet.

The sky is full of sizzling lines of orange light, space

debris falling to the ground so fast my eyes can hardly take it in. Not a comforting sight. Only some of the debris is on fire, though—most of it is huge boulders that are merely smoking.

The others need to be warned. If they come outside in this, they could be seriously injured or worse. Taking a deep breath, I start yelling.

"Stay in your buildings!" I shout, raising the volume on my voice as high as it can go. "Do not go outside! It is a meteorite shower!" I add for good measure.

I see a door open some distance away, but then shut as my voice reaches the occupants of that building. I yell the warning twice more before retreating inside. I hope everyone heeds my warning. It is the best I can do for now.

I return to the bed to hold a now wide-awake Penelope.

"What do we do?" she asks, leaning into me, the pelting continuing like thunder all around us. She winces as a particularly earsplitting crash reaches us.

"We wait. There is nothing else we can do until it passes," I respond grimly. I do not like the feeling of helplessness, but this is something we cannot fight.

The actual duration of the event is almost half an hour, but I stay inside with Penelope for ten more minutes after the noise stops before it's safe enough to look outside and check on everyone. When we open the door, it is clear right away that major damage has occurred even in that relatively short amount of time.

People start to venture out as we do, surveying the damaged buildings, the rocks embedded in the ground. Roofs have collapsed, doors are gone, walls have crumbled. All told, three of the buildings are completely destroyed. Apart from that, there is the relatively minor damage where sections of roof are missing, holes have appeared in other walls, and smaller debris has nicked at countless objects as far as the eye can see.

"We need to reinforce the functional buildings to avoid this happening again," Jackson comments, his eyes somber as he surveys the damage with the rest of us. "With something strong. Perhaps with metal and stone."

Those around us agree with the sentiment. It is a sound one. I nod with the others.

"There is an ore called breksa that may be helpful," I say. "As well as metals deep in the body of Tajss, though I am unsure if they can be found in the mine."

"Then we have to intensify our investigation of the mine," Jackson says immediately. "If there is something useful down there, we need it now."

"That's too dangerous," Penelope interjects. "Bashir is more familiar with Tajss and stronger—it makes more sense for him to go first, so he can navigate the tunnels and map them out for the others."

"I agree," I chime in, smiling at Penelope when she straightens with pride at my support. "The mine work should be delayed until I can go in and check for the possibility of internal damage from the meteorite shower."

"We cannot afford to wait to fortify our buildings," Jackson counters, exasperation clear in his voice.

"It is not safe," I repeat. "Sections could cave in. Waiting for a short period is only prudent in this case."

Jackson shakes his head again, his jaw stubbornly set. His ego is obviously at the wheel again. I attempt again to change his mind, but I am not successful. He stubbornly refuses to entertain my arguments.

"We're going in," he finally says, holding his hand up to stop my words. "That is non-negotiable. And it is not your decision to make."

I shut my mouth. He is right. I am not the head leader

here. When he sees I am done speaking, Jackson turns to the villagers and raises his voice to tell them his plan.

"We will go into the mines! We will find the ore and metals we need to fortify our buildings..." he announces.

I shake my head as I watch him orate. Jackson seems possessed with the need to maintain his authority, to raise the spirits of the upset villagers. The latter is commendable, but I suspect Jackson believes the ores he might find could give him the power to dictate to Rosalind. He would love to be in a position to tell her what to do and so have more to offer the New Villagers.

I fear his impatience may result in more trouble than good. Rushing in to something of this nature without proper planning is foolhardy. Those involved in the mining effort push forward, but they look at me when Jackson tells them to move out. They heard my opinion when I gave it, or it reached their ears at some point. With so many people in close proximity, news travels. Also, I was not trying to be particularly quiet, especially towards the end.

"We need the metal and the ore," Jackson says sharply, obviously also noticing the looks, and not appreciating the lack of respect for his authority.

They murmur their assent and move toward the mine after that, none of them protesting. The uneasy feeling in my stomach tells me this is a bad idea. I can only hope I am wrong.

"You tried," Penelope reassures me, her eyes also worried as she watches them leave.

I nod my assent and put my arm around her shoulders as we turn away, back to our quarters. Sometimes trying is not enough.

The suns are high in the sky by this time, so we go about our daily activities, but it is not long before we hear word back from the mines.

"Jackson! Jackson!"

Penelope and I both rush out of our quarters, as do the other New Villagers when we hear the shouts. I can see right away that there is nothing we can do to help.

The group that entered the mines has returned, their clothing and faces smeared with dust, carrying the blood-stained body of a fallen comrade. Jackson rushes over, his face white as he takes in the body.

"What happened?" he asks hoarsely, his face haunted.

"There was a sudden collapse when we tried to push through a section," the one in front explains grimly. "Otis was caught in it."

The head injury is clearly what killed the poor man. Everyone gathers around, stricken by the sight of the body. Anger flares inside me at the loss, at the unnecessary death.

The mining crew picks up Otis's body and carries it to his quarters. A minute or so after they enter, a long, hoarse, woman's scream pierces the air. Everyone looks in that direction. The screams continue.

The woman's grief makes me furious. Knowing that the man died to satisfy Jackson's need to establish dominance has me desperate to change this situation. The New Villagers need to circumvent their own egos and learn to listen when they are warned by a native who has their best interests at heart. That is the moment Elmer decides to use this tragedy as political capital.

"This is unacceptable!" he shouts, drawing the attention of the shocked and grieving crowd. When he sees he has every-one's attention, he throws his shoulders back, the gleam in his eye indicating he's enjoying the attention. "Jackson is ill-prepared to be the mine leader!"

The screams go on and on. A woman in the crowd kisses her man's cheek and then heads towards Otis's quarters. Restless movement in the square and people's murmurs have

Jackson glaring at Elmer. But he does not return the volley, whirling and rushing away instead.

I frown. It is difficult to deny the claim when we just saw the casualty. Even more difficult to deny it when I too think he holds some responsibility for the death. But to run away?

"Where is he going?" Penelope asks, frowning at his back.

"I do not know." I tighten my arm around Penelope. Everyone is holding someone, a friend, a lover. The grief we can all hear reminds us: death is an unexpected visitor.

The last scream tapers to a moan, and then there is silence from Otis's quarters. Bless that woman who went to her friend.

"*I* will bring back what we need!" Jackson announces as he hurries out of one of the buildings and then turns away. He has a laden bag across his back. Supplies?

"Shit," Penelope mutters, taking a step towards him.

I follow her, hurrying to catch up with Jackson's fast-retreating form.

"What are you doing?" Penelope demands as we draw even with him.

"I need to fix this. Without endangering more lives," he says shortly, his face tight. "I need to show them that I can take care of them." Distraught and wracked with guilt, he is not thinking clearly. Again.

"Rethink this plan," I try again. "You will be in just as much danger—"

"I don't care!" Jackson retorts, aiming a glare my way. "I'm going in. It's not your decision."

When we reach the mine entrance, he does not hesitate. He disappears into the darkness immediately.

I clench my jaw, turning to Penelope. I know what I have to do, but I do not like having my hand forced in this manner.

"Penelope, I have to—"

"—go in after him," she finishes for me with a slight, tight smile. I can see she is as angry as I am. Rising on her toes, she kisses me hard and fast. "Be careful. Oh, and take this." She hands me a pen and a notebook. She always has something to write with. I take them from her carefully.

"You are a treasure indeed," I murmur, not referring to the objects, but to her understanding of the situation, her support.

"Just come back in one piece," she retorts, her gaze serious.

I nod, stepping towards the entrance, looking back once to burn this picture of her into my heart.

"I will," I promise. I want to linger, but there is no time to waste. Jackson will not be moving at a sedate pace, not in his emotional state.

Taking one of the discarded torches at the entrance, I light it and follow Jackson quickly. My greater stride has me upon him in little time, the light from the entrance quickly disappearing as I follow the turns. The fact that the tunnel he has chosen is blocked by a pile of rock also aids my quick closing of the distance between us.

"Come," I order Jackson, leading him in another direction. "We will need to take the smaller tunnels to avoid the collapses."

Jackson nods, more open to listening to me now that we are in the tunnels themselves. Now that the danger is real, perhaps. We keep moving. I do not want to be in here longer than necessary, but we must find a balance between speed and safety.

As we walk through the maze, we have to find new routes multiple times. Some of the collapses blocking our way look fresh, likely caused by the meteorite showers, while others appear old. I make a note of the various veins of metal and ore that we do see. More than once, I have to hold Jackson back from rushing forward and accidentally falling into cracks that have opened in the ground.

"Watch the ground," I warn Jackson yet again.

He nods, obviously shaken. Another time, I stop Jackson at my side and hold a finger to my lips, backing up slowly. The tunnel is riddled with the vampiric sismis, their silhouettes only clear once we are almost inside, the ceiling covered in them. At the entrance to another tunnel, I spy a glowing pair of eyes. I do not know which creature it is, but we may not need to take this tunnel. Better to try another and avoid a fight in the small confines of these underground paths. Without room to maneuver, we are more vulnerable than we would otherwise be.

At that point, Jackson is staying fully behind me, following my lead. At least his good sense eventually asserted itself. When we turn into one of the smaller tunnels, Jackson accidentally hits the side when he trips over a rock.

"Careful—" I start, but then push Jackson back quickly when a cracking sound comes from the rocks above our heads. The space where we'd been quickly fills with heavy rocks as the tunnel collapses. The structure was so sensitive that Jackson's fall was enough to destroy the delicate balance inside. We manage to avoid injury again.

Jackson stares as the dust starts to settle, his mouth open, eyes wide.

"Be careful where you step," I say. It's something of an understatement, but if being nearly crushed by unknown tons of rock won't make him slow down and watch the ground, what will? I leave the tunnel to find another to search now that that direction is also impassible.

He nods, closing his mouth and swallowing. He's more careful after that. Slowly but surely, we start to map out a way to the main veins.

One that will not get *anyone* killed.

CHAPTER FIFTEEN

PENELOPE

I sniffle, wiping at my nose. Picard mewls next to me, licking at the tear tracks on my face, the tiny wet tongue tickling me. I chuckle, gently pushing her small face away.

"Enough crying, huh?" I ask, my voice hoarse. Sitting up, I settle her onto my lap, taking solace in her soft fur and warm body. She's helped me through more than one crying jag. "You're right. It isn't accomplishing a damn thing."

I know that, but I keep succumbing anyway. Bashir and Jackson have been gone for too long. Long enough that I've gone through every possible scenario that could end up with them hurt. Or worse. The first time I finally gave in to my need to cry, Picard showed up, big eyes watchful as she crept closer. Maybe it was stupid to project feelings onto an animal, but I couldn't help but feel that she was concerned for me.

If nothing else, her presence had forced me to get up and scrounge up some food for her and distracted me from the ever-constant worry that has plagued me the whole time Bashir has been gone.

When did I become this dependent on him? Become this attached? I don't know, but there's no denying the depth of feeling I have for him after my reaction to his absence. He could hurt me. Really hurt me. It frightens me to think about it, but not seeing him again scares me more.

"Thanks for taking care of me, Picard," I murmur, rubbing her small back. "What do you say we go check on the mining entrance again, huh?"

Maybe it's stupid to constantly go check, but I can't help myself. The best I can do is limit it to a few times a day, when what I really want is to camp out in front of it. Maybe I would if Tajss was a safer place, but staying out there alone at night would be like dangling bait out for sharks to chomp on.

I get up, put on my shoes, and head out of our quarters, Picard on my heels. I'm getting used to her being there. People call out their greetings, and I raise my hand in response, but that's all. I don't have it in me right now to make small talk, to pretend that I'm doing okay. I can't take the sympathy either. I can see it lurking in everyone's eyes. It's well-meaning, but it still grates.

You have to come back, Bashir. That's our deal.

I hold on to that promise as the hours and then days pass. I know Bashir will do everything in his power to make sure he doesn't break a promise to me. He's honorable down to his very bones, a gentleman in the truest sense of the word.

When I reach the mining entrance, Tessa is already out there waiting too. She gives me a wan smile, shrugging.

"Figured I may as well check again," she explains sheepishly.

I smile back, my own expression just as lackluster.

"Yeah," I agree, leaving it at that.

I sit down next to her. Picard roams the area around us, checking back in when she feels like it. Time passes without any kind of sign that Bashir and Jackson are anywhere near coming back out.

Tessa finally gets up to go take care of duties that have fallen on her now that Jackson isn't there any more to oversee things. She gives my shoulder a comforting squeeze as she leaves.

"Don't stay out here alone too long," she warns. "Or I'll have to send someone to get you."

"I won't," I promise.

I wait a little longer. Until it's time to eat again, my stomach rumbling in complaint. I sigh, standing up. I'll just grab a quick—

I hear a scuff of sound. Nothing loud, but different enough that I turn, my heart beating fast.

Is it...?

Picard runs mewling across the mine entrance, something she hasn't done before. Her tail stands straight up, and she stares into the darkness.

I freeze, my eyes trying to make out something, and then I see the most beautiful sight in the world.

Bashir carefully walks out of the dark mine, his eyes squinting to adjust to the bright suns.

He looks tired and dirty. But he's in one piece. That's all I care about.

Before he can fully acclimate to the change in light, I'm wrapped around his tall, strong body, my arms and legs hugging him close as I pepper kisses on his face. His arms come up to cup my backside, hold me up.

"Penelope," he murmurs, moving his face until he can catch my mouth in a proper kiss.

Gripping his head, I pour all my worry, all my relief into that kiss.

He's back.

He's okay.

Everything is going to be fine. The relief sends a trembling wave through me. I break the kiss as Bashir starts to walk with me still in his arms.

"What took you so long?" I demand, wiggling down. I don't know if I want everyone in the village to see us like that, even if they know we're together.

"We wanted to get an accurate map, one that the future miners could depend on," he murmurs, his eyes devouring my face. "It took some time to get through all the tunnels. There were a lot of dead ends and a lot of backtracking involved."

I don't know if it's possible to be more impressed than I am. They came back in one piece. And they have a map?

Jackson grins at my shock. It's the first time I've even noticed him.

"Mission successful," he says with a grin.

Before I can ask any more questions, my alone time with the two of them is over. Someone cries out, alerting the whole village that Jackson and Bashir have returned, safe and whole. The entire population of the place rushes out to greet them. The cheering is loud and boisterous, Jackson soaking it in with a big smile.

"Thank you!" he cries out. "Let's have a feast to celebrate!"

A little self-aggrandizing, but okay. Preparations immediately start for a hearty dinner, the New Village alive with purpose again.

It comes together quickly, and I don't get a chance to be alone with Bashir beforehand. Too many people want to talk to him. I feel my frustration rise, but I also understand. I'm proud of him too.

At the dinner, Jackson stands to give another speech, his glowing face giving away how successful he was in his endeavor.

"I am certain you are all wondering what Bashir and I

found down there in the mines," he starts, acknowledging Bashir with a nod. "Well...it's everything we could have hoped for. And more." He pauses as people start clapping and stamping their feet, smiling at the gathered crowd. He's practically glowing with his victory. When the noise dies down a little he continues. "The ores and metals we've found are, indeed, valuable. Valuable and useful." The crowd goes wild again. "This is a new day for the New Village!" Jackson cries out over the roar, which only increases with that proclamation. "Let's eat!" he yells, throwing a hand up in the air, and deciding that's enough speechifying for the dinner.

Hmm.

As I dig into the food, I can practically feel the renewed faith in Jackson as a leader. The mood is happy, with people finally looking to the future with bright spirits rather than the desperation, mourning, and fear that has colored their mood every day. This means more than the actual find in the mine. Jackson has managed to give them the priceless gift of hope.

Though, practically speaking, much of his success in that arena is owed to Bashir. I doubt he would have made it back out alive if Bashir hadn't run in after him. Though I suppose I'm thankful Jackson gave him a chance to begin with. That was no guarantee. He could have completely rebuffed us both. Still...

Bashir's face appears pensive too, despite the celebration going on around us. I lean in closer, keeping my voice low.

"I'm worried what will happen here when we leave," I whisper.

Bashir nods slowly, looking over at me.

"I am too," he murmurs.

That's...unusual. He hasn't admitted concern until now. Now I know I should be worried. Bashir leans even closer to me, turning his head so his lips brush my ear when he whispers. I shiver at the touch.

"There are more veins that lead towards the Tribe. I didn't put them on the map. Whether the New Villagers agree to co-ownership or not, Rosalind can have access."

Oh. Secret veins? I look back at Jackson, still soaking in the glow of his success. I'm even more worried now. If he doesn't have sole control of the mine, this isn't nearly the coup he believes it to be.

I sigh. That isn't something I can control. We can only do so much. At the end of the day, our loyalty isn't to Jackson or the New Village. Not when push comes to shove. Still, I can't wait to leave the dinner. So I sit just long enough to be polite, eat my food. And then I take Bashir's hand.

He looks over at me, a question on his lips.

"I want to be alone," I whisper, tugging him to his feet. "Come on. Let's get out of here."

Heat immediately replaces the question in his eyes, and then he's the one pulling me along back to our quarters. Neither of us can get back fast enough.

The celebration is great, but it keeps me from showing any of my true emotions, keeps me tethered to a polite face when that's the last thing I want to adopt right now. As soon as the door closes, I push Bashir farther into the room, and then onto the bed. I'm straddling him in the next instant, ripping off his clothes and smoothing my hands over his body while he lies there and allows me to do whatever I want, his eyes heavy lidded.

I don't have the patience to wait. Maybe later, when I don't feel quite so desperate to reconnect. I yank my own clothes off as he watches, his eyes raking down my naked body. His desire for me is clear. It always is. I never doubt his attraction to me. Getting back on top of him, I immediately grab hold of his thick cock and point it straight up. I don't need any preliminaries.

"I want you inside me," I mutter, hovering above him.

"Then do it," he says, his voice raspy as his eyes meet mine.

I moan and he groans as I take him into me in one fell swoop, wanting him deep inside as quickly as possible. It's a tight fit. He's long and thick and I'm tight, but we manage it, until I feel so full, I can feel his pulse deep inside me. Then I brace my hands on his strong shoulders, my eyes on his, and ride him. My hips move hard and fast, the need inside me not anything soft and gentle. My anxiety and worry doesn't leave room for that.

I cry out with a sharp orgasm. Bashir makes a hoarse sound under me as he follows me, but then he immediately flips us over, and his second cock slides right back into me.

"Everything is fine," he murmurs, kissing me gently now, smoothing my hair back from my sweaty face. "I am whole."

I squeeze my eyes shut tight at the soothing murmur, the gentle way he's touching me, until I feel myself start to believe the words he's saying, until I'm calming, despite myself. Only then does he start to move inside me, the rhythm of his hips as soft and slow as mine was fast and hard. The explosive sex gives way to a comforting meeting of bodies. They meet my needs in different ways. Help me connect and ground myself.

"I will keep you safe," he whispers in my ear, his body rubbing against mine as he moves inside me. "Trust me."

I shudder, my hands tightening on his hips. I believe him. I believe him. That trust helps me sink deeper into the pallet, calms me even more, until I feel something...him. I feel Bashir. But it isn't his body. Not his body alone anyway. It's more than that...his...spirit?

I don't know what else to call it, this hazy taste of him

that I can sense inside me. Whatever it is, I can feel it mingling with mine. With the me inside my own body, merging even as our physical bodies are merging. It feels surreal, supernatural.

I trust Bashir. I trust him with more than my body. So I yield to it, ready for whatever he has to give me. I'll take it all, take all of him. I kiss the side of his neck, pushing my face into the sweaty hot skin there that smells like him.

"I'm yours, Bashir," I murmur, taking in a shuddering breath as another orgasm sweeps through me, tingling and gentle as well. I am sure of my words. Surer than I've ever been of anything in my whole life.

"But don't scare me like that again," I add, a warning tone in my voice. "I won't stand for it."

He chuckles, nuzzling my throat.

"I will not."

And then he proceeds to love me until I don't have a stiff bone in my body.

Well.

Not counting his anyway.

CHAPTER SIXTEEN

BASHIR

*T*he next day, it is finally time for us to leave. A great deal has happened in the time we've been here. I do not know how much actual progress we have made, though we are coming away with valuable information.

Penelope and I pack quickly, our belongings sparse, light enough to travel with. Jackson and the New Villagers all gather to wish us luck, and I do not doubt their dismay at seeing us leave. Though how much of it is personal to us and how much is their knowledge that they have no way to source food without us is up for debate.

"You are welcome to stay as long as you would like," Jackson reiterates, even though Penelope and I are ready to go, our belongings with us as we say goodbye at the edge of the village.

"Thank you," I respond gravely. "Your hospitality will not be forgotten."

"We appreciate it," Penelope agrees. "But we do have to get back to the City. Then back to our home."

Jackson nods.

"You are welcome back at any time."

There is a hint of the same trepidation we are feeling about leaving Jackson in charge alone reflected in his eyes, though he hides it well. Perhaps the glow of the mine victory has started to fade. But he cannot always depend on us to prop up his role here. He needs to find out one way or another if he can hold his position, and if he is strong enough and a good enough leader to deserve the role. It sounds harsh. But Tajss is a harsh land.

We thank him again and wave at the gathered villagers. There are people I will miss, people who were kind to me, to us. But this is not where we are meant to be. We have people to get back to.

So we walk away, start on our journey, Picard running along beside us, in front of us, or behind us, depending on the mood she is in. We do not get very far before Penelope brings up her concerns about Jackson.

"What will happen now that we're gone?" she asks, glancing over at me. "How are they going to take care of themselves? Is he going to be able to hold on to his leadership role?"

All valid questions. I can see she wants reassurance.

"It will be all right," I say, considering my words. "Jackson is learning his limits. If we stayed, there is the possibility that people may start looking to us for guidance, and that is not why we were there. It is best Jackson have influence over the New Villagers."

"What about Elmer?" Penelope prods. "He doesn't look like he has any intention of quietly allowing Jackson to lead."

I sigh. Good point.

"Elmer has designs that do not bode well for anyone," I admit. I can feel that truth in my bones. "But that does not mean he will succeed."

She nods, though I can see she still worries. I understand.

There is no guarantee of things working out how we want them to. We can only hope they do. There is just so much we can control.

We move on to a different topic. I do not want to dwell on the negative, so I begin to tell her about some of the flora that we see, sporadic though it is in the heat. I know this is just the kind of thing she likes to hear. Interestingly, there is not much movement as we travel. Tajss is mostly quiet on the surface.

"I believe it is because the creatures are frightened," I explain when Penelope brings it up. "Even a deadly thing knows to duck its head when rocks fall from the sky above."

The red, rolling sands are more peaceful than she has likely ever seen them. I see her relax into the quiet of it, and I am glad for it. She has been under a heavy load of stress, as have I. Spending this time simply bonding with my treasure sounds wonderful. Away from everyone, from the various responsibilities and requests. Here, it is just us. It is nice.

We talk and learn more of each other as we travel, stopping periodically to rest and take care of our needs.

"You have to give me some space," Penelope says, shooing me away.

I do not want to leave her alone, but I understand her need for privacy too. So I compromise. I move off just far enough that I cannot see her, but I can hear her cry out for help if she needs it. She takes care of her business quickly, and then we are moving forward again.

It does not take me long to realize something is wrong. I glance behind my shoulder again, feeling that sense of unease that lets me know all is not well.

"What is it?" Penelope asks, looking over her shoulder as well in response.

I catch a small glimpse of a humped back a few dunes away, the creature out of sight again in the next instant.

"A guster," I respond grimly. "It is clearly in pursuit of us, though I do not know why."

Not a random encounter like the previous one was. It appears too focused, following our trail exactly.

"A...guster?" Penelope repeats, going pale. "Oh...no."

I turn to her.

"What?" I ask, hearing more than the usual alarm in her voice. "What is it?"

Swallowing she reaches into one her packs and pulls out a guster egg.

"I found them when I had to...go. I figured the beast wasn't around, so it was probably hunting far away..."

I shake my head. No wonder it was after us. We had its eggs!

"That was a mistake," I say mildly, my mind running through our options at this moment. Again, I would rather avoid conflict with Penelope here with me. Her safety is paramount.

"Quickly—pick Picard up," I order, dropping one of the bags we are carrying.

I keep two of them, but that third will weigh me down. It contains surplus meat, but we should have enough to make it to the city. If not, I can always hunt.

Penelope rushes to pick Picard up, and I sweep the two of them into my arms, moving the bags to the side to distribute the weight more evenly. It is cumbersome, but the best I can manage.

The guster crests the nearest dune, its eyes focused on us, razor-sharp teeth on display.

We left the cart in the village, so we are not tethered to this spot as we were in our previous encounter. Time to take advantage of that fact.

"Hold on," I mutter under my breath.

Penelope tightens her hold on me and on Picard.

Flaring my wings, I leap, using them to increase the distance I can travel.

Then again.

And again.

Penelope holds on tight, her grip on me and Picard turning white-knuckled.

The guster cannot travel as fast as I can leap with the aid of my wings, and it will have a difficult time tracking us now that we are landing only after significant distances. Still, I make sure to travel even farther than I need to, to make sure we are no longer being pursued before I touch down to the sand for good, just to be sure. I will not take a risk with Penelope.

On the last leap, I kiss Penelope hard, judging it safe to speak now.

"Why would you steal guster eggs?" I ask her, shaking my head.

She shrugs, clearly embarrassed at the mistake.

"I hear they're really good, and I thought—"

"You did not *think*, love," I interrupt, amused even in my horror. "It is never a good idea to steal guster eggs, or babies from any creature for that matter. They do not look on the theft lightly."

"That's for sure," Penelope agrees. "I'm sorry. I won't do that again."

Picard chooses that moment to mewl as well, though the sound is low. Clearly, the kedi knows to act with caution, taking its cues from us. It will make a good pet. It did not even make a fuss when it was grabbed and held for so long, clearly sensing there was danger nearby.

Once we've landed for good, Penelope lets the small creature go, and we continue on our journey once more.

My wings have taken us quite close to The City and The Tribe, so we have some time to stop and eat. Tajss is again still and mostly quiet around us. Though the guster encounter has me watching with increased awareness.

"It looks like an '80s sci-fi movie decorated with ornaments," Penelope comments.

I take in the scenery. Meteorites and stormglass litter many of the red, rolling sand dunes surrounding us.

"Is that good?" I ask, taking another bite of meat as I consider the sparkling sand.

She nods, her eyes sparkling just as brightly as our surroundings.

"It's quite beautiful, actually," she says, sighing happily as she feeds Picard another bite. "It looks...festive. And happy."

"Hmm."

I cannot look away from her glowing face. She is the one who is beautiful. A treasure who deserves *all* the treasures. I make a note of her reaction. Another clear example that shows she likes shiny things. I could stay there like that with her forever, watching her enjoy our surroundings. But we soon have to move forward again, the call of duty and responsibility too strong.

Even closer to The City, Penelope needs to take care of her needs again.

"We are almost there," I point out, not wanting to take another risk if we do not have to.

"I can't wait that long," she insists, dancing in place. "I'll be quick!"

Amusement has my mouth turning up at the corners, even as I feel a twinge of apprehension in my gut.

"Do not come away with anything that does not belong to you," I warn, relenting.

She nods enthusiastically.

"Don't worry—I've learned my lesson," she agrees.

I do believe she has. I nod and she leaves, hurrying.

"Do not wander too far," I call after her.

"I won't!" she calls back.

My unease grows as she leaves my sight. Sighing, I sit down in the sand, Picard joining me a few feet away.

"Just a little longer now," I comment to the creature, who tilts its head at me. "We're almost there."

I sigh again. I do not like having Penelope out of my sight, but—

A scream has me leaping to my feet.

"Bashir!"

Penelope! Hearts pounding I turn towards Penelope's voice, running and leaping forward using my wings, Picard running at my side in the same direction, her sleek body surprisingly fast. Fear is an icy finger down my back as I crest the dune in her direction.

Penelope is struggling on the sand, iridescent green vines wrapped tightly around her, from her thighs up to her shoulders, more slithering around her as she continues to struggle. The nadzem vines will squeeze her to death if I do not get them off her.

I want to run over and cut through them all, pull her out of their grip. But that might take too long, might end up with me trapped as well. Not helpful for Penelope. I take a deep breath, stilling my body so I can think more clearly. I cannot make a mistake here. Penelope could pay for it with her life.

"Bashir!" she screams again, her calves now also covered in the vine.

Picard mewls anxiously, hesitating as she sees the vines.

Penelope needs to stop struggling.

"You have to stop struggling!" I order in a hard tone meant to be obeyed. "Release your fear—it is reacting to it!"

She gives me an incredulous, desperate look and I can see she wants to argue. Perhaps point out nobody mentioned this in her interviews.

"Please, Penelope," I push, my own desperation making my voice hoarse. "Trust me."

I can almost hear her heartbeat from here, her fear a potent cloud around her. Then she takes a deep breath and trusts me. She closes her eyes, going still. Taking more deep breaths. Her body starts to relax. The pulse point in her neck slows. It takes some time. Long, nerve-wracking moments. Slowly, the vines start to react to her changed state and begin to loosen their tight hold, until space appears between them and Penelope's body.

"I am coming closer. Remain calm," I murmur, carefully stepping through them, keeping my own breathing steady and calm. I could reactivate them again if I am not careful.

Crouching down, my feet in the gaps between the vines, I slowly slide the slack ropes of the plant off her slender body. Her eyes open and she moves her hands to grip mine just as carefully. Together, we slide her out and then carefully walk away, avoiding the tendrils strewn across the sand.

Once we are clear of the danger, I pull her close, my hearts beating quickly, the fear shuddering through my body again, now that I can feel the emotion without repercussion. Penelope holds me back just as tightly, her body trembling against mine as we just hold each other for long moments. Picard rubs up against our legs, her mewls of worry slowly quieting now that Penelope is safe.

"You are not leaving alone again," I mutter into her hair. "You will simply have to hold it. Or go in front of me."

She laughs, the sound a little wet from emotion.

"Copy that," she murmurs, rubbing her face against my chest.

I let out a breath. She may very well be the death of me.

CHAPTER SEVENTEEN

PENELOPE

*W*e finally make it to The City. I am so done with the journey at this point, even though we still aren't at our final destination. Miles and miles of desert and the beating suns have worn me down, despite the company, not to mention the scares along the way.

I'm sure Bashir feels the same after having to come to my rescue twice. How embarrassing. I glance over at his profile. Even if those eggs did turn out to be delicious.

In any case, the sight of The City is a more-than-welcome sight by now. Tension melts away from my shoulders as soon as we're inside, in the safety of the dome.

Picard immediately jumps out of my arms, her furry head raised, little nose wiggling as she sniffs the air. She must smell Sarah. She turns to look at me, and there's confusion in her eyes, her uncertainty about whether she should stay or go. I feel a pang in my heart, but Picard was Sarah's first.

"It's okay," I murmur, crouching down to be more level with her. "Go. I'll see you again."

Seeming to understand, she hops over to nuzzle against me, the affection welcome. Then she scampers away to follow Sarah's scent, obviously excited to meet her other friend.

"Can we follow to make sure she reaches Sarah safely?" I ask, turning to Bashir.

He gives me a gentle look, nodding.

"Of course."

His hand is a comforting weight on the small of my back. So we follow behind the small creature that has wormed her way into my heart as she makes a beeline right over to Sarah, where she is sitting outside near one of the buildings. She cries out with joy as Picard mewls, leaping into her lap and rubbing her furry head against her face. Sarah looks up, her eyes searching.

"Thank you!" she calls out when her gaze lands on us, her joy easing the slight ache in my own heart. "Thank you so much!"

I'm so happy we could do this for her. We smile and wave back before moving forward again.

We need to check in with Rosalind. She needs to know what we know. We ask around until we find out where she is. When we finally track her down, her assistant has us wait for bit until she's done with another meeting. After all that, we're allowed in to see her while she's having her dinner.

"Penelope, Bashir! I'm so glad to see you both back, healthy and in one piece," she greets us, her smile wide.

I can see that she is truly, sincerely pleased to see we've made it back. I understand the sentiment. There were several times when escaping with our lives was not a guarantee. Of course, nowhere here on Tajss can be well and truly safe. Everything is just degrees of dangerous.

"Please, have a seat," she urges, gesturing to the chairs across from her. "Welcome back," she adds before getting right to the point. I don't blame her—she's always been the busiest person I know. Efficiency is necessary. "How did it go?"

Her tone is lighthearted, but there is tension in the room and lurking behind her eyes. It's been there since she learned that Gershom's followers came into possession of their very own village. I don't know how she's going to react to the details of what happened.

"Jackson was somewhat reasonable...at least after Tessa convinced him to let us stay..." I start out.

Somewhat reasonable is the best I can do while describing Jackson's behavior. He doesn't come out smelling like a rose when we go through everything, but that isn't because of our retelling. Bashir takes over the tale in some parts as we piece together the entirety of our stay in the New Village.

There is a lot to get through. Rosalind's face remains impassive throughout, even when we touch on Jackson's view of her and her offer of cooperation. Even when we discuss his hidden plan with the mine, his desire to use it as leverage against her. Despite her lack of outward reaction, I can't imagine that grandstanding and rebellion is going to go over well with Rosalind.

She listens quietly, letting us say everything we want to. When we're done, it's clear we didn't manage to make it to the point we all hoped we could. The New Village is still a thorn in our sides, despite our best attempt to make inroads.

"You have a map of the mine?" Rosalind asks Bashir when it's clear we're at the end of the narrative.

"Yes, I made a copy including the veins of ore that lead out," he hands over the folded piece of paper. "Jackson has the map omitting those particular veins."

"Excellent," she murmurs, looking at the map.

When she's done studying it, she nods, lifts a piece of meat, and takes a bite. She chews on it contemplatively, her thoughts turned inward. Bashir and I look at each other, waiting for her reaction. After a few minutes of thoughtful silence, she puts down the food and leans forward.

"They'll come to their senses eventually. With these meteorite showers, they may not even have a village to hole up in soon. So I imagine this will all sort itself out." She sits back in her chair again. "The two of you should go take a load off—eat, rest. You've done good work here. The lack was clearly not in you or your approach." She holds up the map. "And I look forward to putting this map to good use, Bashir." She meets both of our eyes individually. "I want to reiterate—you've both done exceptionally well. I thank you for your service."

"Glad we could help," I say, standing up at the clear dismissal.

Bashir murmurs something along the same lines. And then we're out of there.

"That was interesting," I say to Bashir in a low voice as we head out of earshot.

"Hmm." He looks over at me. "Let us see what she does with the information."

I agree. Rosalind liked to play things close to the vest. Her actions would tell the true tale. Now that I've actually gone to the New Village, seen the people there, the problem seems much more real than it did before. I feel more invested now in the outcome. I know those people. They aren't all bad. Far from it. But we played our role, at least for now. We're going to have to just wait and see like Bashir says.

"Can we check in on Sarah?" I ask, switching gears.

Bashir nods. So we head back over to her. When we find her, Picard is still ballistic with glee, so ecstatic to find her human that she's practically bouncing off the walls, filled with energy. Sarah laughs as Picard weaves through our legs and then zips away to circle her again.

"I can't thank you enough," she gushes. "Picard has brightened my day so much."

I grin at the little creature's antics.

"She's adorable," I agree, sitting down. "She would brighten anyone's day. She certainly did mine."

Sara nods happily.

"True. But enough of Picard—what's up with you guys?" she asks, shifting the conversation. "How was the New Village?"

So we hit the highlights again with her, laying out all the trouble we encountered with the New Villagers. We didn't go into as much detail as we had with Rosalind, keeping it to what we thought were the most relevant points. Sarah nods, a slight frown between her brows.

"It doesn't make much logical sense, but logic and reason aren't always what dictate our actions, huh?" she murmurs.

"This is true," Bashir agrees. "And not simply for humans."

Sarah chuckles at that, nodding.

"Too true. It's probably a problem with any and all sentient beings."

Bashir leans forward.

"I believe that is a fair assumption," he agrees. "I am sorry, but I have to know—do you have any news of the Tribe?" he asks, switching gears again.

She nods.

"These meteorite showers are a complication nobody saw coming, but I hear the Tribe is fine. They sustained some damage, but not to anything crucial. The people are all fine."

Oh, good. That's really good to hear. Bashir relaxes next to me at that news as well. Something else has been bothering me as well though.

"What about the City?" I ask. "It doesn't seem to have sustained any damage, at least not any that I can see. And those meteorite showers are no joke. We've seen what kind of damage they can do."

Sarah nods.

"It missed us altogether," she explains. "The shields somehow altered the course of the meteorite showers away from us here. We never felt any of it."

That is not the answer I was expecting. Though I had no idea what I *was* expecting.

"Wow," I mutter. "That's convenient."

"That it is," Bashir murmurs, looking thoughtful. "Very useful."

That's all the time we have for that conversation as others start to drop in to visit Sarah.

At one point, Drosdan gets food and brings it over so we can all eat and discuss everything that has happened. The conversation is lighthearted, but also serious as we all consider the future.

"The New Village will have to soften their hard stance," Drosdan comments as we eat. "They do not have the strength or the resources to sustain it."

"Yes," Sarah agrees, followed by murmurs from everyone.

I sigh internally. Too bad everyone but the New Villagers themselves can see the writing on the wall. I just hope they don't realize the obvious only after it is too late.

CHAPTER EIGHTEEN

BASHIR

"We are so happy to see the two of you mated," Drosdan remarks as we get ready to leave, the murmurs of agreement from those assembled warming my heart.

"It's really great! I'm so happy for you!" Sarah gushes, hugging Penelope tightly.

Penelope laughs, hugging her back, a flush of embarrassment coloring her cheeks at the attention, but she smiles at everyone as well. I bring our clasped hands up to kiss the back of hers.

"I am happy as well," I murmur, looking into her warm eyes.

The flush in her cheeks deepens further, and I just want to be alone with her, safe in our quarters, where I do not have to worry about any impending danger, or people watching, or anything but the two of us. Penelope seems to be of the same mind. We say our goodbyes and leave the small social gathering, walking back to our quarters, her small hand still gripped in mine. The walk feels long, though it takes only minutes.

Once inside, it is as if a weight has been lifted of my shoulders. No guster to watch out for. No people to impress or convince. No need to keep my hands to myself.

"I'm so glad we're done with our part," Penelope admits with a sigh as I pull her into my arms and wrap my wings around her for good measure. I cannot have her close enough.

"Yes," I agree. "I do not envy Rosalind her responsibilities."

It is true. Our aspect of this was specific, bound by certain parameters. Rosalind needed to actually fix the problem. And failure was not an option.

"Hmm." Penelope cuddles in closer. "I completely agree with that. I don't know how she handles the stress. I'm just so relieved we're finally safe."

It is an echo of the very thing I was thinking.

"Come," I say, letting her go to take her hand. "I think you will feel even better after a bath."

She smiles, allowing me to pull her over to the small bath. I turn on the water to fill the tub and turn back to help her undress. She watches me as I draw the dusty garments off her.

"What about you?" she asks as I guide her over to the now full tub.

"I will take care of myself after you," I murmur, helping her lower her lovely body into the steaming water. "One moment—I found something else for you."

I find my pack and pull out the fragrant sprigs I picked for her on the journey back. Her eyes light up as I rub them in my hands and drop them into the water, their fragrance drifting up to fill the room.

"They smell wonderful," she sighs, leaning against the side of the tub, her eyes closing in pleasure. "You're going to spoil me Bashir."

I smile, soaking a washcloth. I lift her leg out of the water, draw the washcloth across her glowing skin in small circles, making sure to clean every inch.

"You deserve to be cared for," I murmur. "In fact, there was a time, according to the ancient writs, when women were actually 'prayed' to. If I understand the meaning of the word."

"They were?" Penelope asks lazily as I switch over to her other leg.

"Hmm. The men cared for them properly, as they should. And there was a sense of peace on Tajss." I draw the cloth up her flat stomach, across her delicate ribs. Over the tight points of her breasts. She sucks in a breath at the gentle touch. "Even the beasts mostly minded their business," I murmur, absorbed in the task of sliding the cloth over her body.

I look up when her hand covers mine.

"I'm sorry your women did not survive," she offers in a low voice, her eyes filled with empathy.

I smile, squeezing her hand. She is truly beautiful. I knew that her physical body was pleasing to the eye from the moment I saw her, but I find that the beauty she holds inside far surpasses even that.

"I am honored that you are mine," I say softly, leaning down to kiss her gently.

"I feel the same way," she murmurs, cupping the side of my face, her eyes filled with emotion.

I kiss her again. I cannot help it. The kiss deepens. My hand slides under the water to touch her, caress her. My palm slides over her easily under the water. I finally break the kiss, wanting more, wanting all of her.

She wraps her arms around my neck as I lift her from the bath, ready to take her to bed. Her lips press into my jaw with small, suckling kisses. I suck in a breath. I want to make love to her—

"Everyone—come to the city center! We want everyone present for an announcement!"

I freeze with Penelope in my arms as the shout reaches us from the hall.

"What is that about?" Penelope wonders out loud, looking over at the closed door.

I shake my head, at a loss myself. I do not know. But we need to go find out.

Mood shattered, we get ready to leave quickly.

By the time we make it to the center, a crowd had already formed, and Rosalind is on a raised platform with her mate Visidion at her side.

She is already speaking as well.

"...why you are all here now." She scans the crowd. "I want to be clear and transparent with everyone here because you choose to follow me as your leader, and I feel I owe it to you." Murmurs of agreement among those watching. Penelope grips my hand. "We are having problems with the New Villagers. They do not want to cooperate with us, do not want to form an alliance. This is dangerous for all of us on this world—conflict and ill will is the exact opposite of what we need to survive." She glances at Visidion. He gives her a slight nod before she continues. "It seems as though the relief we have generously provided the New Village may have also succeeded in blinding them to that reality of life on Tajss. So. I do not think this one-sided relationship is in our best interests. If the New Village does not sign on to a trade agreement, does not agree to cooperate with us...we will stop sending supplies."

The murmurs are louder this time, more energized, but they do not sound like protests. As I look around at those assembled, I feel that deep down...many feel that she is correct. As harsh as this measure would be, it is not unjust.

Gershom caused a great deal of trouble, and even after

that, Rosalind sent his followers aid despite the animosity between them. What did those followers do? They spit on that helping hand. Spit on the City and the Tribe even as they took what was given. Hypocrites.

"She's not wrong," Penelope murmurs next to me, echoing my own train of thought.

I voice my own agreement. Once the reaction settles, Rosalind continues.

"I want to have control of the situation, to ensure this does not escalate. I also believe the ores in those mines they have access to should be co-owned, not hoarded as leverage to be used against us. So I intend to show them the error of their ways through delayed supply runs until they pledge to work with us and agree to co-ownership of the mines. Once they agree...they can again continue to enjoy the meat and fruits the Tribe grows and so generously shares."

With that, Rosalind steps down and sweeps away, the announcement finished.

I understand this approach and the reasoning behind it.

I only hope nobody gets hurt in the process.

CHAPTER NINETEEN

PENELOPE

"*I* don't know. Elmer is an idiot and Jackson is often illogical. I'm not sure either of them will take the reasonable path here, no matter how beneficial or necessary for survival."

I make a frustrated sound.

"You're not wrong," I agree. "But we can't make their decisions for them. There is nothing to do but wait. And hope."

"Yes, your concern is understandable," Bashir chimes in. "Perhaps Rosalind will allow an entourage of Zmaj to go offer the New Villagers who would like to leave one final chance to choose a saner place."

Sarah nods, not looking convinced.

"I hope it won't come to that," she murmurs, petting Picard where she's curled up in her lap. "Maybe they'll come to their senses."

I agree with that sentiment. I don't think any of us want it to come to that. But if the New Village has already held out this long...

And with Jackson and Elmer involved in a stubborn power struggle...

I just don't know.

In a perfect world, both of them would only have their people's best interests at heart. But this isn't a perfect world.

"There is no use in worrying," I add, standing. "I know that's easier said than done, but it's still true."

Sarah smiles wryly, nodding.

"True." She sighs, seeing Bashir stand as well. "It's fine. I know you guys have to get back to the Tribe."

"We'll visit again soon," I reassure her, stepping close to hug her.

She hugs me back.

"Have a safe journey back."

We say goodbye to Drosdan as well. He's been quiet and watchful during the conversation, which I'm sure he's already had with Sarah. It's a complicated situation, one that we're all worried is going to blow up.

I know my own advice is true. There is no use in worrying. We'll have to deal with what happens when it happens. Obsessing over it doesn't actually accomplish anything. I have plenty of time to think about it on the journey back to the Tribe. It's a struggle to keep my mind from picking at it, but I manage.

"I am so tired of traveling," I groan when we're halfway there.

Bashir chuckles.

"I agree. But this is the last leg of our journey. We are almost there."

True. I think I would be happy not to go anywhere for a few months though. I'm bone-deep exhausted in a way that one night's rest won't even make a dent in. By the time we do arrive, it's nearing dark, and we're just in time for dinner.

"Welcome back, guys!" Delilah exclaims, the others also getting up to hug us, slap Bashir on the back.

"Have you news?" Melchior asks as we all sit down to eat.

"Yes," Bashir says, launching into the details. "The New Villagers are not ready to cooperate with us and Rosalind..."

He lays out the big points, and we both fill in the details as people throw out questions.

"So Rosalind has decided to withhold supplies if the New Village does not agree to terms?" Ormarr reiterates.

"Yes. We're all hoping it doesn't come to that, but..."

It's clear we've laid out an accurate picture when there's a moment of silence where everyone just chews. With all the information on hand, it doesn't seem as if the New Village will just agree. I push that thought aside resolutely. Not focusing on that. Not focusing!

I finally take a bite of the special sauce Delilah has put out, curious to see how it turned out. And to distract myself. My eyes widen as the flavor bursts in my mouth.

"Delilah, I don't know how you did it, but this is even better than before! I didn't even know that was possible!"

She grins at me.

"Tajss had to give us something good, right?" She winks at me. "We'll liven it up around here if it kills us."

I laugh, my heart warming at the good-natured return. It's so good to be back. There's been so much to process over a relatively short amount of time that I feel exhausted. I'm just glad to be back here.

Back...home. Not just the cut-and-dried meaning of the word. It truly does feel like that, surrounded by the dragon I love and the friends who are my family. Surrounded by people I care about and who care about me.

I reach out and take Bashir's hand. He smiles at me. After everything...

I'm not going to take this for granted anymore. Or only see the negative. There's a lot of good here too.

I focus on eating as I consider that.

Until the talk turns to the meteorite showers, again grabbing my attention.

"According to the old writs, the storms usually precede certain events that change the course of history," Melchior explains.

"Yes," Ormarr agrees. "There are multiple recorded examples, including when the zemlja almost died, when the oases tripled in number..."

He goes on to list more examples. It's quite a list. Melchior strokes his chin.

"Soon, the world may be a very different place than the one we have become accustomed to." His face and his tone are serious. Foreboding. "We simply do not know if it will be for good...or for ill."

"I'm hoping it'll be for the good," I interject into the silence. "At least the stormglass is pretty."

That elicits chuckles, breaking some of the tension.

"It is gorgeous," Delilah agrees. "Maybe even useful." She stretches her arms behind her head. "I'm not worrying about anything tonight. I'm just glad the two of you are back, safe and sound."

There's an enthusiastic round of agreement from everyone else at the table at that sentiment, filling my heart.

Home.

I've found it after all.

CHAPTER TWENTY

BASHIR

"*A*re you sure this is going to be worth it? You know I'm tired of traveling. I'd be ecstatic just to stay in one place for a while."

I chuckle, continuing forward with Penelope held securely. When I told her I had a surprise I wanted to show her, she'd looked at me seriously.

"I like surprises and I don't like surprises," she'd said.

"You'll like this one," I promised, hoping I was right.

And I know the reason she does not like surprises is because she likes to be in control. The fact that she trusts me enough to let go is a gift in itself.

"It is going to be worth it," I reassure her. "You will see."

I've been excited about this since I secured special clearance to take the short trip with Penelope.

"All right," she sighs leaning against my chest as I continue to use my wings to travel quickly. She gives me a side-eyed look. "So...has anyone else seen this surprise?"

"No," I reply honestly. "I only ever wanted to show you."

I can see her soften at the words—and it is true. The sand cave is among the very few treasures I keep private. But I do not want to keep anything private from Penelope. I want to share everything with her. Everything I am and everything I have.

Over the years, I've collected and stored a variety of things there, but even more importantly, it is the first place I remember after emerging from my Bijass. Much of what came before this place is a blur. This cave...it is the first clear memory I have. It is precious, a link to my past that I keep secret, hold close. Protect. Now I want to share it.

Luckily, the trip itself is short and there is no trouble along the way, though I remain alert for the possibility.

My next flying leap has us landing directly in front of the mouth of the cave. The suns are at such a point in the sky that light shines far enough from outside that we can see a fair amount even before stepping inside.

Penelope's eyes widen with delight as I carefully set her on her feet.

"Bashir...it's gorgeous," she whispers, staring.

I smile, looking from her to the entrance of the cave. The opening is a broad, curved arch, the walls ridged as they expand back into the dune itself. Inside, holes in the ceiling let even more light stream in, highlighting some of the treasures I keep inside. I step forward with her as she stares in wonder.

"I have cataloged years of finds," I explain. "Objects, ancient relics, books written in sacred symbols..."

She shakes her head as she enters, her fingers skimming one of the books before moving on to a mosaic bowl, and then on to a heavy cloak I hung on one side.

"I feel like a kid in a candy store," she says, grinning as she looks over at me. "Candy is a sweet treat," she explains before I can ask.

"Ah," I nod, pleased at the description. "I am glad."

Pleasure suffuses me as she continues to explore, interest

and curiosity in every touch. Until she finally turns to me, her expression serious.

"I'm honored that you've brought me here, allowed me to see your secret place."

"I would not want to share it with anyone else," I say with a smile.

I trust her. With my heart and with this place. Her answering smile is as filled with love as mine no doubt is.

When she turns away to look at a small, detailed box, I know this is the opportunity I have been waiting for. I take the necklace I made for her out of my pocket.

"I have something else for you too," I tell her, stepping close.

She turns with a question on her lips before her eyes fall on the gift and widen.

"Bashir..." she whispers, shaking her head, her eyes shining as she stares at it. "It's gorgeous."

I traded some of my stormglass for sparkling, deep green ores from a New Villager. Drilling holes in them carefully, I had then strung them along some smooth twine to create the jewelry.

I gesture for her to turn around. She does, and I carefully fasten the piece around her slender neck. It looks as though it belongs there.

"It is a token of my mating claim," I explain, leaning down to lay a soft kiss on the side of her neck.

She turns to me, blushing, as she skims her fingers over the eye-catching necklace.

"I hope you will see you as I see you," I add, cupping the side of her face, the green of her eyes so much more beautiful than my gift. "Precious. Blooming under pressure. A reflection of my heart."

"Oh Bashir," she responds, blinking back tears. "I love it. It's absolutely perfect. And I love you."

She rises up on her toes to kiss my lips with her soft ones. The heat that flows between us now is tender, sweet. I slide my hands down to her hips, and carefully guide us to the plush pallet I have set up on one side.

Sighing, she drops down onto the softness, holding me close when I come down on top of her. We touch each other slowly, savor each sensation as if we have all the time in the world. In that hidden place, just the two of us, it feels as though that is possible. Our clothes come off leisurely, until skin slides against skin, until I cannot resist the hot temptation of her body any longer. When I slide into her warm clasp, I am home.

She is mine.

And I am hers.

I kiss her as I move in her, the softness of her body cradling mine so perfectly. Her face is flushed, her bright hair sticking to it as she gives in to the passion. She is so beautiful. I can watch her like this forever. When the pleasure finally overtakes her, she cries out into my mouth, her fingers gripping my shoulders. Her climax brings my own. I shudder above her, the release deep and more meaningful than the physical act itself.

I will never grow tired of her. I love everything about her, but most of all I love her spirit. And that will never change. Afterwards, we eat the food I brought with us, exchanging kisses and caresses that keep the heat simmering at comfortable level.

Then I show her the small, clear spring. She delights in playing in it with me, laughing and splashing me, her happiness making my own chest feel full. Until I have to touch her again. Kiss her again. Make love to her again.

The next few days, all we do is absorb each other. Eat, drink, bathe. And join our bodies. We are almost never not touching in some way. Her hand in mine. Her back against my front as we lie on the palette. Her leg brushing mine in the water. I feel drunk on her when the end of our time approaches. We hold each other close while we lay on the palette, Penelope tracing my face with her fingertips, her eyes dark and satisfied.

"I don't want to leave," she confesses, her tone tender.

I kiss her fingers.

"I will never forget this time with you," I agree. "It is a wonderful dream that I do not want to end."

She smiles, propping herself up on my chest.

"Yes. But I mean Tajss." I still under her. She does not want to leave Tajss? But she has always hated it here. She smiles at my response. My face likely gave my thoughts away. "I have everything I need right here. And for the first time since I got here...I can't imagine leaving." She searches my eyes. "I love you, Bashir. So much."

Turning us over so she is underneath me, I lean down to kiss her, pouring my emotions into the play of my mouth on hers.

Her words are...everything.

"I love you, Penelope," I whisper, my lips brushing hers. "My treasure."

She is the one I always dreamed of.

But I could never have imagined someone so perfect for me.

THE END

ABOUT THE AUTHOR

USA Today Bestselling Author of fantasy and scifi romance, Miranda Martin's books feature larger than life heroes with out-of-this-world anatomy and smart heroines destined to save the world. As a little girl she would sneak off with her nose in a book, dreaming of magical realms. Today she brings those fantasies to life and adores every fan who chooses to live in them for a while.

She was born and raised in southern Virginia, but as a veteran she's traveled to places like Korea, Hawaii and good 'ole Texas. Now she's settled in Kansas, the heart of America, with her husband and daughters. Her favorite animals are dragons, unicorns and cats. If she's not writing, you can still find her tucked away somewhere with a warm blanket and her nose in a book.

Get in touch!
mirandamartinromance.com
miranda@mirandamartinromance.com

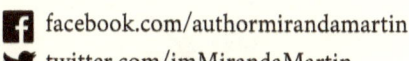 facebook.com/authormirandamartin
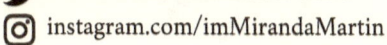 twitter.com/imMirandaMartin
instagram.com/imMirandaMartin

www.ingramcontent.com/pod-product-compliance
Lightning Source LLC
Chambersburg PA
CBHW031201260626
47169CB00004B/1201